Till Tomorrow
Author: John Donahue

The year is 1961 and O.B. (Terrance) has just moved to France with his mom and army officer dad. "Cannonball" Wall is the first boy to befriend O.B. Cannonball teaches him all about aces (friends) and deuces (the kind of kids you want nothing to do with).

Claude the "Clod" is the biggest deuce of all. When O.B. fails to make the baseball team, Claude is sympathetic. O.B. soon learns that Claude is clever and funny. Soon the boys learn of the crisis brewing in Berlin. There is fear that the Russians will go on the defensive and that American army bases in Europe will be prime targets. O.B.'s biggest problem, however, is who is truly his friend, Ace Cannonball or Deuce Claude.

The backdrop of this book is war-torn Verdun, France during the WWI Berlin crisis. Readers will grasp a little of the history of the war and the divide of Berlin while learning the meaning of true friendship. With a reading level of 4-6th grade, this will make a great addition to any elementary library. –Diane Limoges.

Till Tomorrow

JOHN DONAHUE

Till Tomorrow

FARRAR STRAUS GIROUX

NEW YORK

Library of Congress Cataloging-in-Publication Data
Donahue, John, date.
Till tomorrow / John Donahue.— 1st ed.
p.   cm.
Summary: In 1961, newly arrived at the United States Army base near the World War I battlefields at Verdun, France, twelve-year-old Terrence "O.B." O'Brien is torn between the popular boys on the baseball team and a French boy they tease for being different.
ISBN 0-374-37580-1
{1. Interpersonal relations—Fiction.   2. Baseball—Fiction.   3. Battlefields—France—Fiction.   4. Military bases—Fiction.   5. Verdun (France)—Fiction. 6. France—Fiction.}   I. Title.
PZ7.D71473 Ti 2001
{Fic}—dc21

00-52828

For my mother, and in memory of my father

Till Tomorrow

Prologue

The Meuse American Army Base, Meuse, France, 1961

My father stepped out of the car first. He always does. He jogged around the front, hopped over the curb, and planted himself on the sidewalk, his hands on his hips. He stared at our new house for a moment. Then, with a wave of his hand, he motioned for us to join him.

I struggled past a brown garment bag and pushed open the side door with my shoulder. It was hard even to stand. The four-hour drive from Paris had left my back stiff and my legs wobbly. I gulped in a breath of fresh air and turned back to the car. "Come on, Mom."

My mother looked up through a yellow haze. The sunlight had splintered on the windshield, streaking her hair and face with long golden lines. "I'm coming," she said. "You go ahead."

I found my footing and stretched my cramped muscles as I walked to my father.

"Big house, isn't it?" my father said.

I tried to measure our new home with my eyes. It was big. Bigger than the house at Fort Thayer. Bigger than the house at Fort Wallace. Big and long and freshly painted white, with red shutters and a red tile roof. Big and long . . . and empty.

My mother's hand touched my arm. I hadn't even heard her come up beside me. "How do you like it?" she asked.

"Okay, I guess. You like it?"

My mother glanced at the house, then back at me. "Looks good from the outside."

We stood there, the three of us, for what seemed the longest time, looking but not speaking. Finally, my mother's whisper broke the silence. "Do you have it with you?" she asked.

I pushed my hand deep into my pocket and felt the stone. "Yes."

"Do you want to do it now?"

"When you and Dad go inside."

My mother caught my father's eye, and they moved together down the wide slate walkway that led to the front door. My father turned the key. The door clicked open, and they stepped inside.

I stood alone on the walkway, waiting for the door to close. Then I fished the stone from my pocket and turned it over in my hand. There was really nothing special about it. No brilliant colors or markings. No crystals. Nothing interesting in its size or shape. It was a stone like any you would find in a yard or garden—round and gray, the size of a quarter, smooth on one side, rough on the other.

I can't really remember when the tradition started, but my mother had told me the story often. I had just turned four years old, and we were all set to move from North Carolina to Ohio. Everything was packed. Everyone was ready. Everyone but me. I started to raise an awful fuss about leaving my old house. That was when my mother snatched the stone from the ground and pressed it in my palm. "Hold this," she said, "and it will bring the old house with you."

So I held the stone, through that move and three others. It had become a kind of ritual for me. Whenever we moved into a new home, I would take the stone and bury it in the front yard. And whenever we moved out, I would dig it up and carry it with me to be buried again.

I left the walkway and found a place by the steps where the eaves cast a cool dark shadow. I crouched low near a small shrub with yellow flowers and pinched the soil. It was moist and would give way easily. I twisted my fingers into the ground and lifted a clump of earth. Then I placed the stone carefully in the shallow hole and pressed the soil back on top. "See you in two years," I said silently.

1

"At this base," said Cannonball Wall, "there's only two kinds of kids—aces and deuces." Cannonball leaned his huge bristly head toward me. "Know what I mean, O.B.?"

I nodded, although I was not at all sure what he meant. I hardly knew this giant of a boy who was sitting next to me. He had appeared earlier that afternoon at my front door, before the moving men had finished unloading the truck. "I'm Cannonball Wall," he'd announced in a voice too small for his size. "You wanna go to the ball field?"

"Go!" my mother had ordered.

And so I went. Now here I was, sitting on the hard wood of the bleachers, baking in the hot June sun, next to a boy who called himself Cannonball.

Cannonball jabbed a sausage finger at the batter's box. "See that guy?" he asked. A powerfully built boy whose blond hair was spiked in a crew cut was striding toward home plate.

"Yeah."

"That's Stanton Rettig. Coach calls him Sluggin' Stan. He's an ace. Good at everything. Baseball. Basketball. Football."

I watched as Stanton dug his rubber cleats deep into the dry dirt, pulled his bat back, and twirled it in tight circles.

The first pitch came in high and inside, the kind of throw that would have sent me diving to the dirt. But Stanton didn't flinch. Didn't budge an inch. It was almost as if he were daring the pitcher, daring the ball itself to hit him. The second pitch was more to his liking. The ball exploded on his bat and shot over the third baseman's head.

Cannonball smiled. "See?" he said.

"Good hit," I agreed.

Cannonball pointed toward center field. "That's Nick Lucci. He's an ace, too."

My eyes followed Cannonball's arm to the outfield. A short wiry boy was pounding his fist into his mitt. His eyes were locked on home plate, and he was leaning forward on the balls of his feet like a cat ready to pounce.

"I'm good friends with both of 'em," said Cannonball. "We play sports together. Go to the movies and snack bar. Stuff like that."

"You play baseball?" I asked. It was hard for me to imagine Cannonball stuffed into a uniform.

"Course," said Cannonball indignantly. "I'm the best catcher in the American Base League. How 'bout you? You play?"

"Yeah, I play."

"Ever been on a team?"

"Sure. Two summers at Fort Thayer." I didn't tell Cannonball I had been on the junior team. Or that I had spent so much time sitting on the bench I could have hatched a carton of eggs.

Cannonball bobbed his head, apparently satisfied with my answer. "You know," he said, "they're having tryouts for the team next Monday. How old are you?"

"Twelve."

"That's perfect. That's the oldest you can be. I turn thirteen in September, so I just made it. You should try out."

"Maybe I will," I said.

"And you know what else?" said Cannonball, lowering his voice. "If you make the team and the guys like you, maybe you can join the club I'm in."

"What club?"

Cannonball grinned. "Can't say. It's secret."

I couldn't tell if Cannonball was kidding, but I decided not to ask any more about it.

Cannonball and I sat together, listening to the crack of cowhide on wood and watching the small clouds of dust that rose like steam from beneath the feet of the runners. I tried to concentrate on the game, but as Cannonball chattered on, my mind began to drift. I could hardly believe I was here, in another house, in another country. It had all happened so quickly. It was not that I hadn't known we'd be moving. I had known that for months. When your father's in the army, you always move. But the past few days just seemed to have blurred together—my last day of school in Massachusetts, the going-away party, the flight to Paris, and then the long drive through the sleepy French countryside to our new home. Now it was time to start all over.

"Heads up! Heads up!" The shouting jolted me from my thoughts. From the corner of my eye, I saw Cannonball leap to his feet. I looked up in time to see a foul ball hurtling straight for my face. Before I could move a muscle, Cannonball's meaty hand flashed in front of me and swatted the ball away. It bounced off the benches below us and rolled to a stop by the chain link fence near the first-base line.

I let out a long sigh. "Thanks," I muttered.

Cannonball plopped back down beside me. "Gonna have to pay more attention," he said.

I nodded and looked away as my face reddened.

A tall gangly boy wearing a blue beret and baggy brown shorts ran to the fence and grabbed the ball. He cocked his arm and hurled the ball into the air. It soared far over the pitcher's head and bounced by the third baseman. The boys on the field erupted in laughter. "Nice throw, Clod!" the shortstop yelled.

Cannonball chuckled. "Clod's the biggest deuce around here." He nodded toward an ancient-looking church spire that rose above a thicket of trees several hundred yards away. "He's a Frog from the village."

"A Frog?"

"You know, a Frenchie."

I had never heard the word before. "How come they call 'em that?"

Cannonball shrugged. "Who knows? Everyone just does."

I watched the French boy as he walked alongside the fence toward the back of the first-base dugout. He had pushed his hands deep into his pockets and was staring at the ground. "Is his name really Clod?" I asked.

"Nah," said Cannonball. "It's some French name like Claude. But everyone calls him Clod." He giggled. "Claude the Clod."

"Why does he come here?"

"Dunno," said Cannonball, shaking his head, "but he always does. Nobody talks to him 'cept the coach."

"Does he speak English?"

"Yeah. His mom's British. She works at the base. I think she's a translator or something."

I looked back at Claude the Clod. He was perched behind the dugout, his thin arms crossed like sticks on his chest. I made a note in my mind to stay as far from him as I could. I did not want a deuce rubbing off on me.

2

With a sweep of his hand, my father brushed aside the clutter on his desktop. "Come here, Terry," he said, unfolding a crisp map and pressing it flat with his palms.

I threaded my way through the footlockers and moving boxes that had turned my parents' bedroom floor into a maze. My father was still dressed in his summer khaki uniform; as he bent over, studying the map, the new silver eagles on his shoulders sparkled in the bright light. "The information officer gave me a packet of materials to go over," he said.

"More rules?"

"Sort of. But this is a little different. And it's important you listen carefully." My father tapped his finger on the map. "Here's where we are," he said, pointing to an area marked in black ink just east of the city of Verdun, near the little village of Meuse. His finger traced a wide half circle around the base. "You see this area here?"

"Yes, sir."

"It pretty much surrounds us on one side, doesn't it?"

"Yes."

"It's a restricted zone, Terry. And no one—not you, not me, not anyone—is to go in there. Is that understood?"

"Sure." My father seldom gave orders at home, and when he did, it was best not to argue. But I continued to stare at the map. We had driven near the restricted area on the way to the base. There was nothing there. No villages. No homes. Just rolling hills, green and brown woods, and wide fields choked with bright yellow flowers. "Why's it restricted?" I asked.

"Artillery shells," my father said quietly. "Thousands of them." He fixed his pale blue eyes on me. "What do you know about Verdun?"

"Just what you told me before we left," I said. "There was a battle there."

"Well, it wasn't just a battle. Some say it was the worst battle of the First World War. Maybe the most terrible battle ever fought." My father moved silently to the bedroom window and pulled back the thin curtain. It was twilight, and the setting sun had colored the sky purple and red. Long dark shadows crept from the trees along the base road and etched eerie patterns on the recreation fields nearby. In the distance, white lights flickered in the French village.

"Do you see that hill?" my father asked, gesturing toward a black swell in the earth that rose up behind the village.

I nodded.

"Before the First World War," my father continued, "the French built a line of forts around Verdun to protect the area from the Germans. A small fort was built on that hill. When the Germans attacked in 1916, there was heavy fighting there. The Germans captured the hill, then the French won it back. Then the Germans recaptured it and the French counterattacked. Soon there wasn't much left but collapsed trenches and rubble."

"Why are so many shells still there?"

"Before each attack," my father said, "there would be an artillery bombardment to soften up the enemy positions. Tens of thousands of shells were fired, but many never went off. After the war, the French tried to clean it up, but they realized it would never be safe. So they fenced off most of it and left it alone. There are battlefields all around Verdun just like it."

I could not pull my eyes from the hill. I tried to imagine what it had been like forty-five years before, when the two great armies had fought there—the blinding flashes of exploding shells, the clouds of dirt and gas, the thundering of cannons and grenades. The very ground on which I stood must have shaken with each blast. "Why did the Germans want that hill so bad?" I asked.

"For observation and to site their artillery," my father said. "And its capture was part of the German plan to inflict massive casualties on the French."

"What do you mean?"

My father shook his head. "It was the Germans' strategy not only to capture Verdun, but to bleed the French as well.

To draw them into a series of fights here that would kill so many French soldiers they would give up on the war. But Verdun became a symbol for the French. They decided that no matter what the cost, no matter how many lives were lost, they would not let the Germans have the city."

"What finally happened?"

"The fighting went on for months, but the Germans never broke through."

"Did they bleed the French?"

My father let the curtain fall back across the window and returned to his desk. "They did," he said at last. "But they bled themselves, too. There were close to a million casualties altogether."

A million casualties. It was hard for me to comprehend. A million fathers, brothers, and sons had shed their blood here. Finally I asked, "How many men died on that hill?"

"Thousands," my father said grimly. "Many were buried in their own trenches during the shellings." He folded the map and put it in the top drawer of his desk. "You understand how important it is to stay away from there?"

"Yes, sir."

My father nodded and walked to the door. "Come on," he said, "let's give Mom a hand."

"I'll be there in a minute," I said. As my father disappeared into the hallway, I pulled back the curtain. Only a few streaks of red remained in the sky as darkness enveloped the village, and the hill was little more than a vague outline in the night. I shivered. It was not really a hill at all. It was a grave.

3

Staff Sergeant Samuel Moss straightened his shoulders and cleared his throat. "Only fifteen boys can make this team," he said, holding a long piece of paper in front of him. "And I count twenty-one names on this sign-up list. So if you want to play for the Meuse Pirates, you have to show me what you can do today." Sergeant Moss spoke softly for a big man, almost apologetically. But his voice was firm and steady, and it commanded attention.

"The coach played in the Negro Leagues," Cannonball whispered in my ear. "Then he played a year for Cleveland before they released him."

I had been to big-league ball games before. Had even seen the Boston Red Sox play a dozen times in a single season. But I had never been this close to a major leaguer. Sergeant Moss still had the look of an athlete—tall and lean, and broad in the shoulders. It was his arms that you remembered, though. They seemed to have been sculpted from marble, like a statue in a museum. Smooth. Power-ful. Perfect.

The sergeant glanced again at his list. "I see a lot of fa-miliar names here. And a few new ones. I especially want to see how you new boys can play."

"Wait till you see him pitch," said Cannonball, his voice no longer a whisper. "He can throw a ball through a wall." Cannonball chuckled when he realized what he had said.

I clenched my fists. I did not want to be near the plate when Sergeant Moss started firing his fastballs.

"Wall," said Sergeant Moss.

"Yeah, Coach," said Cannonball eagerly.

"When I talk, son, you listen. Okay?"

Cannonball grinned sheepishly. "Yes, sir."

"The following players take the field," Sergeant Moss ordered. "Garcia, first base. Carter, second. DePrado, short. Rettig, third. Lucci, center. Rosenthal, left. Higgins, right."

As Sergeant Moss called each name, a player jumped from the bench, scampered up the dugout steps, and ran onto the field. When the sergeant reached the end of the list, he paused. Then he said, "Wall, catcher."

Cannonball leaped to his feet and pounded his huge fist into the oiled pocket of his mitt. "Ready, Coach!" he shouted.

Sergeant Moss swallowed a smile, then pointed at the lumpy equipment bag near the on-deck circle. "Wall," he said, "I had to call every NATO base in Europe to find a chest protector big enough to fit you. So don't wreck this one."

Cannonball beamed and ran toward the bag.

Sergeant Moss eyed his list again. Every position on the field had been filled. Now it was time for the batters to be called. I held my breath. I did not want to be first.

"Who's Terrence O'Brien?" the sergeant asked.

My stomach tightened. "I—I am," I said.

"People call you Terry?"

"No, sir. Mostly O.B."

Sergeant Moss snatched his glove from the dugout floor, turned, and climbed the steps. I sat dumbly on the bench, afraid to move. Did he want me to follow him?

Sergeant Moss stopped midway between the first-base line and the pitcher's mound. "You gonna be a spectator or a player, O.B.?" he asked. "Pick up a bat and let's see what you can do."

I lifted myself off the bench and walked to the bat rack like a condemned man taking his last steps. A dozen hard-wood bats, some old, some new, were lined up by size. I looked them over, then picked the biggest, heaviest one. It would be hard to swing, but it would give me a better chance to make contact. If I could just get a piece of the ball.

As I walked to the batter's box, Cannonball erupted in chatter. "Hey, O.B. C'mon, O.B. You can do it. You can do it. Send it sailin'! Send it sailin'!"

I stepped up to the plate, not too close, but close

enough so that my bat could reach the outside corner. I pushed my helmet down until it fit snugly, and dug my stubby rubber cleats into the dirt.

Sergeant Moss was leaning forward, the ball hidden in his right hand. "Ready, O.B.?" he asked.

I nodded, gritted my teeth, and waited. The sergeant went into his windup and let loose his first pitch. The ball came in below my knees and smacked into Cannonball's mitt. It was not a fast pitch, but I still couldn't get the bat off my shoulder.

"Good eye!" said Sergeant Moss. "That was way low." He smiled. "I'm a little rusty."

"All riiiight!" Cannonball bellowed. "Good eye, O.B.! Good eye! Good eye!"

I took a deep breath and tried to concentrate, but I found it hard even to look at the mound. Sergeant Moss began his motion and let the second pitch fly. I swung wildly, missing the ball by inches.

"Take your time, O.B. Take your time," Cannonball chirped.

Sergeant Moss raised his glove and pointed it at me. "You want to try a smaller bat, son?"

"No . . . no, this is good," I said. But I realized how ridiculous I must have looked, holding a bat the size of a small tree.

"Well, you'd better choke up some. And get that bat off your shoulder."

I slid my hands up the bat's wide stem, pulled my right elbow back, and lifted the wood into the air. I could feel every eye on the field watching me, wondering what I could do. Wondering if I'd take a place on the team.

On his next pitch, Sergeant Moss did not go into his windup. He stood straight up, like a soldier at attention, and lobbed the ball softly at the plate. A lollipop pitch. I brought my arms forward and swung with all my strength, but the ball glided slowly over my bat and fell gently into Cannonball's round mitt.

"C'mon, O.B.," Cannonball urged.

I could feel the blood rise in my cheeks. I stepped out of the box and wiped my palms on my shirt.

"C'mon, O.B.," Cannonball repeated. "Send it sailin'!"

I stepped back into the box and gripped the bat tightly to keep my hands from shaking. I had to get a hit. I had to.

"This one's coming straight over," Sergeant Moss called. "Don't take your eyes off it, O.B. Watch it come in."

I watched the ball come in. And then I watched the next eight pitches come in. Watched them dance around my bat and thud into Cannonball's mitt.

"Okay, son," Sergeant Moss said at last. "You have a strong swing, but you need some practice. Let's give the other boys a try." He motioned toward the dugout. "Peter Stemmer!" he shouted.

I dropped my helmet on the ground and retreated to the darkness of the dugout. No one said a word as I sat down at the end of the bench. No one came near me. For the next ninety minutes I watched as twenty other boys ran and threw, slid and hit, hoping to be picked for the Pirates. My name was not called again.

At the end of the tryout, Sergeant Moss gathered us all in the dugout. He pulled his list from his pocket. This time only fifteen names would be read. "Lucci," the sergeant began. Then the names streamed from his tongue. "Rettig, Wall, Stemmer, Rosenthal, Garcia, DePrado, Higgins . . ."

I listened as the names were announced, but I knew mine was not among them.

When Sergeant Moss finished reading the roster, he looked down at the worn wooden planks beneath him. "I know that some of you boys are disappointed," he said. He looked up, and his eyes met mine. "But you're all good ballplayers. You all tried hard today. And that's what counts."

"Are you gonna have a farm team this year?" Cannonball asked.

"I was just getting to that," said Sergeant Moss. "For you boys who are new, the farm team is for players who aren't on the regular team. You don't get a uniform, but you can practice with us. And you're expected to show up at every game to help out. That means some time on your part because we have a lot of home games this year. If someone on the regular team moves or gets sick, or doesn't give a hundred percent, I'll call up a farm player to take his place. So if you're interested, let me know." Sergeant Moss smiled. "Thanks for coming. And if I called your name, meet me at my car and I'll give you your uniform."

"All riiiight!" Cannonball exploded.

I stood up and slipped silently out of the dugout. The last thing I needed was to listen to Cannonball celebrate.

Making my way along the first-base fence, I noticed a boy near the gate. He lifted the latch as I approached and opened it for me. "Good try, O.B.," said Claude the Clod.

4

Sleep did not come easily that night. Each time I closed my eyes, a white ball drifted toward me, spinning so slowly I could count the thick red stitches on its cover. I could feel my arms strain when I brought the heavy bat into its swing, and I could hear Cannonball groan when the ball thudded into his mitt. The scene played in my mind again and again. Only aces and deuces on this base, Cannonball had said. Now everyone knew what I was.

I opened my eyes as darkness gave way to light. I pushed myself up and propped my back against the wooden headboard. The windows beside my bed faced east and looked out onto the playgrounds and the ball field. They lay quiet now, but would soon be alive with squalling infants, running children—and ballplayers. I would not be there. I would never go back.

Beyond the playing fields, the orange roofs in the village joined together in a rusty streak. Above them, the thin spire of the church grasped at the passing clouds. Behind the village, in the distance, the sun had begun to light the hill where the great battle had been fought. The hill of the dead. My eyes lingered there, then moved back to the orange-capped houses in the village. For some reason, I wondered if Claude the Clod was awake, too.

"Terry," a voice called softly from the hallway. "You up?"

I turned my head. "Yeah, Dad."

"How 'bout some breakfast?"

I glanced at the clock. It was not yet six. Early for me. Late for my father. This might be my only chance to see him. "Okay," I said. "Be there in a minute."

My jeans and T-shirt were waiting for me on the hooks by my door. I pulled them on, then peeked into the large oval mirror on my dresser. The face staring back at me was the same one I had seen the morning before: the brown hair cropped close to the scalp, the blue eyes, the thin nose twisted slightly at the bottom, even the tiny mole on the left cheek. Everything looked the same, but I knew it was not.

My father was sitting in the breakfast nook, bent over his cereal, when I reached the kitchen. "Got yours there," he said, motioning to a yellow bowl across from him.

I squeezed behind the table, lifted the milk bottle, and soaked the sugared flakes. "Mom up?" I asked.

"Not yet. She's exhausted. She must have unpacked fifty boxes the past couple days. I don't think she's even gotten to the footlockers yet." My father shook his head. "I wish I could help more, but with this new job . . ."

I nodded. Even before his promotion to colonel, my father had often been away from the house. There were always meetings or field maneuvers or war games. But now it seemed that he was never around.

"How do you like the base?" my father asked between mouthfuls.

"Hate it," I muttered.

"You hate it?"

"I can't stand this place, Dad. I want to go back to Fort Thayer."

My father put down his spoon and leaned forward against the table. "What is it you don't like, Terry?"

"Everything!" I blurted. "The kids, the base . . . this stupid house!"

My father did not reply, and the expression on his face never changed. He picked up a heavy black mug and blew across the top. Then he rested his elbows on the table and clutched the mug in front of him with both hands. "Does this have anything to do with your not making the team?"

"No," I said sharply.

"You mean if you'd made the team, you'd still feel this way?"

"I—I don't know."

My father took a sip of his coffee, then set the mug down. "What about this farm team you mentioned last night? It seems—"

"I'm not playing on any *farm* team."

"But I thought it was for boys who needed more practice."

"It's for deuces," I said, my voice rising. "Losers. You don't even get a uniform."

My father shook his head. "I don't think the farm team is for losers. I think it's for players who haven't given up. Who want to keep trying."

"Yeah, right," I mumbled. My father didn't understand. He didn't understand anything. "They're gonna feel like jerks, Dad, every time they go to practice. Every time it's gonna remind them they didn't make the team."

"Whom do you think the boys on the team are going to respect more?" my father asked. "The players on the farm team? Or the boys who never show up again?"

"I don't care who they respect," I said angrily.

My father took one last swallow from the mug and rose to his feet. "Look, Terry, I've never forced you to play any sport you didn't want to. But I know you like baseball. And I think you want to be on that team. If you didn't, this wouldn't be upsetting you. If you need practice, I'll try to get home early some nights, and we can go out—"

"I'm *not* playing on that farm team," I said. "And I'm *not* going back."

"All right, Terry. It's your choice." My father buttoned the top button on his shirt and tightened his tie. "I'll see you when I get home, if you're still up."

I didn't say goodbye. I watched from the corner of my

eye as my father disappeared from the kitchen. A moment later, I heard the front door squeak open, then close. I sat alone at the table, stirring the soggy flakes with my spoon. I had to get out of the house. And I had to get away from the base.

5

The village was not much of a village at all, no more than fifty homes and shops packed tightly around the church and a small square. It was hard to tell where one house left off and another started. All seemed to be made of the same drab gray stone. In the center of the square, pink and white roses bloomed beneath a tall statue of a French soldier. The bronze warrior was hunched forward on a pedestal, his helmet shading his eyes, his heavy rifle clutched to his chest, frozen forever in a valiant charge.

I left my bike near the worn steps that led up to the church and checked the time. Six forty-five. All the businesses were dark except one. At the far side of the square, light filled a tiny shop whose sign read BOULANGERIE. An old man in a white apron was moving about behind the counter. It was worth a look.

I crossed the square and peered through the front window. The store was filled with bread of every description—long thin loaves, fat round loaves, loaves that looked like fingers, loaves that looked like torpedoes, all placed neatly in wicker baskets. And atop the counter, delicate pastries lay in neat rows, one after another, like soldiers on parade. Even from the street, the store smelled delicious.

A bell above the door jingled as I stepped inside. *"Bonjour,"* I mumbled. With that one word, I had pretty much exhausted my knowledge of the French language.

The old man must have guessed as much. "You—you want—" He paused and made a face. Then he said a word that sounded a little like "pan."

"Pan?" I asked.

There was a burst of laughter behind me. I whirled around. A boy wearing a floppy black beret was standing in the doorway, grinning broadly. "Monsieur Girard was asking if you want bread," said Claude the Clod.

The old man smiled. *"Oui, oui,"* he said.

"I . . . I guess so. What do I tell him?"

"Just say, *'Je voudrais une baguette, s'il vous plaît.'* "

"Je vou . . . voudrais une . . ."

"Une baguette, s'il vous plaît."

"Une baguette, s'il vous plaît," I repeated.

"Bon!" said Claude. "Very good!"

The old man plucked a long loaf of crusty bread from a basket and passed it to me. It warmed my hands.

"It costs fifteen cents," said Claude. "He takes French francs or American money."

I fished in my pocket and pulled out the change.

"Merci," said the old man.

"Merci," I answered. I tucked the loaf under my arm and followed Claude to the sidewalk.

"What are you doing here?" Claude asked.

"Nothing," I said. "Just riding around. What are *you* doing here?" I felt stupid the moment the words left me.

Claude smiled. "I live here."

"I mean, what are you doing at the bakery?"

"I live here," Claude repeated. He pointed at the windows on the floor above the shop. "Upstairs. With my mother and my *grand-père*."

"Is your grandfather a baker?"

"No, he used to be a teacher. He owns the building." Claude pushed his hands deep into his pockets. "You ever been here before?"

"No."

"Want me to show you around?"

"I—I got to get back soon," I said, searching for a way to escape.

"Won't take long," said Claude. "There's not much here."

I glanced again at my watch. "Well . . . maybe for a minute."

Claude drew his hands from his pockets and gestured toward the statue in the square. "That's the Verdun soldier over there. It's kinda famous. People come from all over to see it. It's supposed to remind you of the men who fought here." He paused. Then he added, "Like my *grand-père*."

"Your grandfather fought at Verdun?"

"Yes."

"Where?"

"In the trenches near Fort Douaumont. And in a small fort nearby."

"You mean that fort on the hill?"

Claude nodded. "It's not really a fort anymore. It's just rubble and overgrown fields."

"You've been there?"

"No," said Claude. "But my *grand-père* told me about it." He grabbed my arm and tugged me across the square to the statue. When we reached it, he bent over and rubbed his thumb against a flat plaque near the soldier's feet. As a thin layer of dirt disappeared, words began to emerge. *"Ils ne passeront pas!"* said Claude. "Know what that means?"

"No."

"It means, 'They shall not pass.'" Claude rose to his feet and looked up at the tarnished features on the bronze soldier's face. "When the French made their stand here, that became their—" He stopped and searched for the right words. "Rallying cry," he said at last.

A car coughed noisily on the street. I looked over my shoulder. An old French automobile was rattling along the road.

"You want to see the church?" Claude asked.

"Uh, just for a second," I said. At least no one would see us there.

Claude darted across the square and bounded up the church steps three at a time. I followed closely behind. When he reached the door, he pushed himself up on his toes and touched an ugly gouge in the wood several feet above the handle. "Feel this," he said.

I reached up and ran my finger along the jagged edge. The wooden shards pulled at my skin.

"Shrapnel did it," said Claude. "From an artillery shell that went off course. The priest said the war tried to get inside the church. To destroy what was good. But the church wouldn't let it. You believe that?"

"Dunno," I said, unable to drag my eyes from the ugly scar that marred the wood. If a single piece of shrapnel could do that to a door, what, I wondered, could a whole shell do to a man?

Claude grasped the handle with two hands and pulled it open. "Follow me," he ordered, vanishing into the darkness of the entryway.

The church was not like any other I had seen before. The thick stained glass of the windows filtered the sun and created long shadows on the floor. There were no pews, just rows of old wooden chairs and kneelers facing front toward an altar of white marble. And it was cold, almost October cold. My body trembled in a shiver.

Claude grinned and tapped the floor with his sandal. "The stone," he said. "It holds the coolness of the night."

"Is it okay to be here?" I whispered.

"Sure. The priest lets anyone in. And I work here, too."

"You work here?"

"Sort of. I play the organ at mass when my *grand-père* can't make it." Claude turned and motioned toward the balcony behind us. The thin pipes of an organ soared above the railing.

"How long you been doin' it?" I asked.

" 'Bout two years. But I've been playing for six." Claude hesitated. "I'm—I'm doing a concert in August. Maybe you could—"

"I got to get going," I said.

Claude lowered his head. "Okay," he said quietly. Then he led me back to the scarred front door. He pushed his thin shoulder against it and held it open for me. "You going to the game next week?" he asked.

"No."

"You should go, O.B. I'll be there. I do the scoreboard."

"I'm not going," I said again.

Claude shrugged. "If you change your mind, look for me."

"Sure," I lied.

6

The music came from the record player in the living room. I recognized the tune. It was a lively song from a musical my parents had once seen. My mother played it from time to time, but mostly she played it when my father was away and she was sad. I marked the place in my book, swung my legs over the side of my bed, and made my way to the open door of my bedroom. "You okay, Mom?"

I waited, but there was no answer.

"Mom?"

"I'm okay, Terry," a voice finally called.

I hurried to the end of the hallway. The living room was dark save for a funnel of white light cast by the floor lamp near the couch. My mother was sitting in the harsh light, crumpled newspapers spread on her lap, a small cardboard box at her side.

"What are you doing?" I asked.

"Just going through the picture box," my mother said, looking up.

"Can I see?"

"Sure, come sit down."

As my mother shifted to the side of the couch, I took a place beside her.

"Look at this one," my mother said before I had even settled in. She held up a small picture framed in silver. The photograph showed an older man in a dark suit, his arm draping the shoulder of a handsome woman wearing a long flowered dress. "Nana and Grandpa," I said.

My mother ran her thumb gently over the protective glass. "It's my favorite," she said softly. Then she added, "I liked Fort Thayer so much because we were close to Boston. We could see them almost every week."

I reached over and took the picture from my mother's hands. "Maybe they can visit us, Mom."

My mother forced a smile. "It's a long trip, Terry. And they aren't young anymore."

I looked again at the picture, then back at my mother. "Do—do you like it here?"

My mother took a deep breath. "I've always wanted to come to Europe. For as long as I can remember. The castles, the costumes, the old cities. It's been a dream for me." She paused. "But I miss what we've left behind."

My mother lowered her eyes and reached again into the cardboard box. "Look what else I found." She passed a long rectangular picture to me.

Sixteen faces stared out from the black-and-white photograph. There was Stephen Anthony, my best friend at Fort Thayer, his ears jutting like handles beneath the sides of his baseball cap. There was Bernie Kline, grinning as if he'd just hit a grand slam in the seventh game of the World Series. There was Ted Lewis, looking cross-eyed at the photographer, hoping that Coach Jackson wouldn't see him. And there I was in the front row, dead center, gripping a small sign that read: TIGER JUNIORS, FORT THAYER, 1960. "Seems like a million years ago," I said.

"It does," my mother answered.

"We were the worst team ever."

"No you weren't."

I shook my head. "Mom, we lost every game but one. And the only reason we won that one was because the other pitcher kept walking us. Don't you remember how bad we were?"

"What I remember," my mother said, "is how much you loved going to those games. You were dressed and ready to play three hours before they started." My mother touched the photograph. "I think you'll miss it, Terry."

I didn't answer. I didn't want to explain again the difference between the regular team and the farm team. And I sure didn't want to get into an argument about it.

"You should put the Tiger picture on your dresser," my mother said.

"I will."

My mother pressed the newspapers on her lap into a

large ball and placed it on the coffee table. Then she rose from the couch and walked to the wooden console by the window. She lifted the arm on the record player and set the needle in the right groove. As her song began to play again, my mother smiled.

7

The top of the hamburger bun was a blank canvas, and Cannonball, an artist. He carefully squirted a wide red circle of ketchup. Then he squeezed a smaller circle of mustard inside it, making sure the two rings didn't touch. Next he daubed a smidgen of relish inside the mustard ring, giving the top the appearance of a target on an archery range. "Know which snack bar has the best burgers in the States?" Cannonball asked.

"No," I said.

"C'mon, guess."

"I don't know. Haven't been to 'em all."

"C'mon," Cannonball urged.

"Fort Wallace?"

Cannonball flipped the top gently onto the burger and tapped it with his finger. "Not even close," he said, shaking his head.

"Fort Thayer?"

"Nope."

"Fort Carroll?"

Cannonball wrinkled his brow. "Never been there, but I don't think so."

"I give up."

"Fort Lott," Cannonball announced.

"Where's that?"

"Arizona." Cannonball leaned forward. "They got a jumbo burger there where they chop up mushrooms and onions—and peppers. Then they fry 'em all together and put 'em on top with melted cheese. And they got this sauce that they smother on everything. And they're huge, O.B. Twice as big as these." Cannonball stared dreamily into the air, as if he were remembering his best birthday.

I settled back in my chair and looked around. The Meuse snack bar was not as big as the one at Fort Thayer. But then, the Meuse American Army Base was not nearly as big as Fort Thayer. The tables were bright yellow and scrubbed clean. The chairs had high orange backs and wide seats. Carrot chairs, Cannonball called them. In the corner, three young privates were listening intently to a sergeant who seemed to be talking more with his hands than his mouth. Nearby, two girls were bent over the jukebox, deciding which song deserved their nickel. I turned back to the table and watched as Cannonball savored his creation. "Cannonball?" I asked.

"Hummmp," Cannonball grunted, like a lion that had been interrupted with its kill.

"How come they call you that?"

"You mean Cannonball?"

"Yeah."

It must have been the one question that could keep Cannonball from his food. His lips split in a wide grin, and he put down his burger. "You haven't seen me at the pool yet," he said. He pushed his chair back from the table, lifted his knees, and hugged his legs with his arms. "Cannonballllll!" he shrieked.

The entire snack bar broke out in laughter. Even the serious privates in the corner could not resist a chuckle.

Cannonball unwrapped himself and glanced at the clock above the long counter. "Wonder where the guys are."

I checked the double glass doors. No one was there. I almost hoped it would stay that way. "Maybe they aren't coming," I offered.

Cannonball shrugged. "Who knows? They keep forgetting they're supposed to meet me." No sooner had Cannonball said the words than the doors swung open, and Stanton Rettig and Nick Lucci stepped into the snack bar. Both were wearing tan shorts and red-striped T-shirts, as if they were in uniform. Each carried a small gym bag in his hand.

"Over here!" Cannonball bellowed.

Nick raised his hand in a wave, then fell in behind his friend. When they reached us, Stanton eased into the chair on my right, and Nick sat on my left.

"Where you guys been?" Cannonball asked.

"The pool," said Stanton, "checking things out." His short blond hair was wet and matted across the top of his forehead.

"Yeah," Nick added. "Checking out those sisters who moved in last month."

Cannonball bobbed his head excitedly. "The twins? The twins? Next time, come get me, okay?"

Nick shook his head. "Cannonball, we want to meet 'em, not scare 'em."

Cannonball ignored Nick's remark and gestured toward me. "You guys remember O.B.?"

"Yeah," said Stanton, "we saw him at the tryout."

I felt my face flush. In the days since the tryout, no one had said a word about how badly I had played. Not Cannonball. Not anyone. I had hoped it had all been forgotten.

"You play any other sports?" Stanton asked.

"Sure he does," said Cannonball.

"Like what?" asked Stanton.

My mind raced. "Well . . . well, I play basketball."

"You any good?" asked Nick.

"He means, do you play basketball as good as you play baseball?" Stanton smirked.

I swallowed hard. They knew I wasn't the greatest athlete. But I was not about to let them make fun of me. "No," I said, staring Stanton straight in the eye, "not nearly as good."

"Not nearly as *good*?" Stanton asked, puzzled.

"Nah, baseball's my best sport. Can't even hit the backboard in basketball."

Stanton held my gaze for a moment, then his lips crinkled in a smile. "You got me," he said.

I let out a deep breath. My joke had worked.

"I told you guys he's okay," said Cannonball, beaming. "Maybe we can let him in the club someday."

Stanton's smile turned to ice. "You know the rules, Cannonball," he said.

"Just—just asking."

Stanton leaned over and picked up his gym bag. "Let's get outta here, Nick," he said. He pushed back his chair and stood up. "And *you* keep quiet," he warned, wagging his finger at Cannonball.

"Yeah, yeah," Cannonball mumbled.

Stanton took a step toward the door, then stopped. "You going to the game Thursday, O.B.?" he asked, glancing back.

"Dunno," I said.

"You should think about it."

I nodded. And as I watched Stanton and Nick disappear through the door, I wondered what kind of club would not let its members speak. What club was so secret its existence could not be known?

I pulled a sheet of white paper from the top drawer of my desk and placed it squarely in the center of the wide writing blotter. Then I picked up my pencil and turned it in the hand sharpener until the clear plastic case was filled with light brown shavings. There was a lot I wanted to say in my letter, so I didn't waste any time.

Dear Nana and Grandpa,

Well, I'm in France now. It's kind of a strange place. On the base, it's just like living in the States. They have a neat pool, a movie theater, and a snack bar. But if you go off the base at all, everything's really different. The French have these little tin cars that rattle down the road. And the kids wear sandals and berets.

For a moment, I thought of telling my grandparents about Claude and how he had shown me his village, but I decided not to.

I pressed the pencil in my fingers and continued:

I've met some boys already and a kid named Cannon-
ball who lives down the street. He's really funny and we've
been to the snack bar and the ball field.

The ball field. I looked up from my desk at the Tiger
Juniors photograph on my dresser. The team seemed to be
staring down at me, watching me as I wrote. I sighed. My
grandfather loved baseball. Loved it so much he used to
drive from Boston to Fort Thayer just to watch me sit on
the bench. I knew he would want to know about the base
league and how I was doing.

I tossed my pencil down and leaned back in my chair.
How could I tell him? How could I say I hadn't even
made the team? I glanced again at the photo. I remembered the bright summer day it had been taken and how
happy I had been. My mother and father were right. I did
like baseball, and I wanted to be on a team. My thoughts
turned to Stanton, Nick, and Cannonball. Would they
think more of me if I was on the farm team—or if I hung
my head and never went to another game? I knew the answer to my own question.

I took a deep breath, picked up my pencil, and leaned
forward.

There are two kinds of baseball teams here. There's a
playing team and there's a farm team for the other players.
I'm going to be on the farm team, but the coach says if you

practice really hard you might be able to move up to the
playing team. Don't worry, I'll make it.

I smiled. It felt good to write the words. I finished the
letter by stating simply:

I really miss you both and I wish I could see you.

Love, Terry

I stopped writing and skimmed over my letter. I added
the following words:

*P.S. We get all the baseball scores here, Grandpa, so I
know how the Red Sox are doing.*

My grandfather would like that.

While I folded my letter, I heard a soft knock, and my
bedroom door opened.

"Are you finished?" my mother asked, stepping in.

"Yup." I pushed the paper into the envelope, moistened
the flap with my tongue, and pressed down hard to seal it.
I passed the envelope to my mother.

"Do you want to come with me?" my mother asked.

"To the post office?"

"Well, I was going there first, and then to the chapel."

"The chapel?"

My mother nodded. "I told Father Quinn I'd help
arrange the flowers for the altar."

The last thing I wanted was to listen to my mother talk to the base chaplain. "No, thanks, Mom. I'll stay here."

"I'll be back in about an hour," my mother said, stepping into the hallway.

I got up from my desk and dropped onto my bed. I lay back, put my hands behind my head, and closed my eyes. The farm team. It was not where I wanted to be. I decided then and there that I would do whatever it took to make the real team.

9

The wooden bleachers rumbled beneath the stamping feet, and the air shook with cheers and clapping. It was almost time for the first pitch of the first game of the new season. I stood on the dusty path that skirted the stands and watched. Cannonball was hunched over on the top step of the dugout, tugging furiously at a thick canvas strap on his shin guard. Behind him stood Stanton, his dark blue cap pulled to his brow, his uniform as white as the Arctic snow. Across the field, a sea of light gray uniforms surged in the visitors' dugout. It was now or never.

I crossed over to the gate in the fence, lifted the latch, and stepped onto the grass. Cannonball must have seen me coming. "O.B.!" he yelled. "Over here!"

I took a deep breath and jogged to the dugout.

"Didn't know you were coming," said Cannonball.

"Just wanted to wish you guys luck."

"We don't need luck," said Stanton, winking. "We need a new catcher."

I glanced down into the dugout. Sergeant Moss was sitting at the end of the bench, scribbling in a notebook. "O.B., isn't it?" he said, looking up.

"Yes, sir."

"What can I do for you?"

"I—I was thinking maybe I'd join the farm team."

Sergeant Moss flipped the notebook shut and stood up. "Good! You're the only boy who's shown an interest so far. You want a job?"

"Yes, sir."

The sergeant climbed the dugout stairs and scanned the field.

"What about the scoreboard?" Stanton asked. "The Frog's not here."

Sergeant Moss pressed his lips together tightly and leaned over until his mouth was near Stanton's ear. "I don't *ever* want to hear you call him that again," he said quietly. "You got that straight?"

Stanton bowed his head and looked away.

The sergeant shaded his eyes with his hand and squinted at the huge black scoreboard behind the right-field fence. "Where is Claude?"

"Probably got lost," Cannonball muttered.

Sergeant Moss shot a hard look at Cannonball. Then he put his hand on my shoulder. "I promised the French boy he could keep score, but he hasn't shown up yet. Think you can handle it?"

"Sure," I said.

"Then get going, son."

I turned and started to run toward the thick green grass that carpeted the outfield.

"Wait!" Sergeant Moss ordered.

I stopped and spun around. The sergeant was rummaging through a large green duffel bag. "Here it is," he said. He flicked his wrist, and a blue cap sailed through the air. I snatched it and turned it over in my hand. A white "P" was stitched above the brim.

"You work hard," said Sergeant Moss, "and you'll get the rest of the uniform."

"All riiiight!" Cannonball shrieked, like a high-pitched whistle.

A grin tightened my cheeks. "Thanks, Coach," I said. I tugged on the cap and set off for the right-field fence. I climbed over, then pulled myself onto the wooden plank beneath the scoreboard. I pushed aside a rusty metal bucket filled with pieces of white chalk and settled in. It had to be one of the best seats in the ballpark—five or six feet in the air, and no one sitting in front of me. I rubbed my finger against the blackboard. It was dry and would show the chalk well. I turned back to the field, and waited.

"Hey!" a voice called. "Hey! Oh Beee!"

My eyes darted to the right, toward the village. There, no more than thirty yards away, was Claude, bounding through the high grass. His thin arms poked like pipe cleaners from the sleeves of a red plaid jacket, and a black tie flapped at his neck. His head swam beneath a red beret.

"Oh Beee!" he called again.

I could do nothing but stare as Claude drew closer and closer. When he reached me, he threw himself waist-high onto the plank and extended his arm. "Give me a hand," he grunted. I took his wrist and pulled him up onto the plank.

Claude sat for a moment, panting like a tired dog. Then he said, "Almost didn't make it. Got stuck at the church playing at a wedding."

"The coach told me to come out," I said. "I'll see if he wants me to do something else." As I leaned forward to push myself off the plank, the stands erupted in applause. The Meuse Pirates were streaming from the dugout like bees from a hive. The game had started. It was too late to ask the sergeant.

"How do you want to do it?" Claude asked.

"Do what?"

"The scores. You want to do the Pirates or the Sabers? Or do you want to do one inning and me the next? Or do you want to do the first three innings and me—"

"What difference does it make?" I snapped.

"Okay," said Claude, "you do the Pirates."

I watched from the corner of my eye as Claude yanked off his clip-on tie and unbuttoned the top button on his shirt. He folded the tie carefully and placed it between us. "Want to hear a funny story?" he asked.

I looked at him but did not respond.

"Last year," said Claude, "in the game against the base at Bar-le-Duc, I got the scores all mixed up. Every time

Bar-le-Duc got a run, I marked it in the Pirates' box. And every time we got a run, I put it in Bar-le-Duc's box. Everyone was yelling at me. The players. The ump. The people in the stands. It was really funny."

"You—you think that's funny?" I asked.

Claude nodded. "Kinda."

"What did Sergeant Moss say?"

"He couldn't stop laughing. Told me as long as I kept giving the Pirates extra runs, he'd keep me doing the score."

I shook my head. Something was not right with Claude. Something under that bright red beret was a little mixed up. But it was hard not to smile. I could almost picture him, dressed like a clown, marking the wrong score on the board, inning after inning. Maybe it *was* funny.

For two hours, Claude and I sat together, watching each pitch and marking each score. We saw Cannonball smash a ball so far over the left-field fence no one could find it. We saw Stanton Rettig drill three singles into center field, each hit as crisp as the creases in his uniform. And we watched Luis Garcia and Tom Higgins ground into double plays. All the while Claude babbled on—about the village, his grandfather, his school, his cat, but most of all, his music. I listened politely but said little. There was really no point in talking. After the game, I probably wouldn't speak with him again.

When the sixth inning was over, we looked back at the

board. Four runs for the Pirates, five runs for the Etain Sabers. We had lost our first game.

"Tant pis," said Claude, tossing his chalk into the bucket.

"What?"

"Means 'too bad.' But they'll win next time. You'll see."

I slid off the plank and dropped to the ground. Claude landed beside me. "What are you doing tonight?" he asked.

I shrugged. "Dunno."

"You want to come to my house for dinner?"

"I—uh—"

"Only for an hour," said Claude quickly.

"I—"

"C'mon, O.B."

Finally my mouth opened and I spoke a word I did not want to say. "Okay."

10

The room was tiny, not much bigger than a walk-in closet. There was a bed, neatly made, pressed against the right wall, and a small desk and chair pushed against the left. In one corner, a tall floor lamp stood guard over a wooden bookcase that was crammed with sheet music. In the other, clean clothes were piled in a wicker basket. Claude pushed open the heavy white shutters on the window. "Smell this," he said.

I grasped the sill and leaned outside. Sweet smells from the bakery below still lingered in the warm air.

"Sometimes in the morning," said Claude, "my room smells like the *boulangerie*. You can't get it out of your clothes. When I go to school, kids call me the baker boy."

"That's not so bad," I said. "I mean, it's not like living over a dump or something."

Claude smiled. "I think some people on the base think this whole village is a dump."

I didn't answer, but I thought of Cannonball and Stanton.

"They're wrong," said Claude. "Meuse is a good place to live."

We stood at the window and watched the darkness consume the last pink shades of sunset. As the square below us dissolved in deep shadows, my eyes were drawn to the bronze soldier. He looked different now, in the dim light. More like an animal, crouched, and ready to pounce. "It must have been awful here during the First World War," I said.

Claude nodded. "Very awful." He pulled one of the shutters closed and turned. "You want to see something?"

"Sure."

Claude dropped to his knees and groped under his bed. A moment later he dragged out a long cardboard box and lifted the cover. "Here," he said, holding up a rusted chunk of metal as if it were a priceless relic.

"What is it?"

"Part of a canteen," said Claude. "From the battle."

I took the canteen and turned it carefully in my hands. The metal, or what was left of it, was paper-thin and covered with a thick brown grit. Tufts of dried moss clung stubbornly to the drinking stem. "What's this?" I asked, pointing to an ugly gash near the bottom where the metal was splayed inward.

"Bullet hole," said Claude solemnly.

"Where'd you get it?"

"My *grand-père*."

"The hill?"

Claude nodded. "He went there last month. He goes every year to plant flowers."

"How come?"

"I think so the dead soldiers will have a beautiful place."

"But it's off limits," I said.

"Not for him," said Claude. "He's been going there forever. He knows where they cleared some of the shells away." Claude paused, then said, "After the war, he and the priest used to go every Sunday and collect the bones."

"The bones?" I was not sure I had heard Claude right.

"There were thousands of bones up there. Still are. They put them in baskets and brought them to the *Ossuaire* at Douaumont." Claude must have guessed I didn't understand. "There's a huge monument right outside Verdun," he explained, "where they keep the bones of all the soldiers they couldn't identify. You can look through little windows and see them. It's almost like—like a church. A sacred place."

Claude reached back into the box and carefully lifted a dark lump. "Bottom of a German boot," he said. "It's still got some hobnails on it."

I returned the canteen and took the lump from Claude's hand. It was hard to believe. A soldier, probably a young soldier, had once worn this boot. I ran my fingers over the dirty studs. How had he lost it? Had it fallen from his pack? Had he taken it off to rest? Had he—I felt a chill creep up my back—had he worn it on the day he had died? I dropped the boot back into the box.

"I got more stuff," said Claude. "I got a cartridge box and part of a—"

"No, that's okay," I said. I stood up and turned away. There were several photographs on Claude's desk. In one, a young man with black hair slicked back from his forehead was holding a scrawny child in his arms. At the man's feet lay a huge white dog. "Who's this?" I asked.

Claude pushed the box back under his bed and climbed to his feet. "Me," he said, pointing to the dog, "before I was handsome."

I grinned.

"Actually," said Claude, "that's my dad and me. And our dog Chaser. We used to call him the dumbest dog in the world because he chased his tail until he collapsed."

"Where were you living then?"

"Indochina."

"You lived in China?"

"Not China," said Claude, smiling, "Indochina. The part we lived in is called Vietnam."

"Oh yeah," I said. I vaguely remembered the name. There was some kind of fighting going on there.

Claude lifted the picture and held it in both hands. "My father works for the French government. He was sent to Indochina when it was under French control. We lived there till the Communists made it too dangerous. I don't remember much about it. 'Cept how green it was."

"Where's your dad now?"

"Algeria. We lived there for a little while, but it got dangerous, too. So my father sent us to live with his father—my *grand-père*. Been here two years now."

"When's he coming back?"

Claude shrugged. "Maybe six months. Maybe a year. The Algerians want their independence from France. There's a lot of trouble there. But he'll come back soon. Then we'll be a family again."

There was a sadness in Claude's voice that I had not heard before. He was almost like an army kid. Always moving. Always starting over. Always wondering if his father would be safe.

Claude replaced the photograph on his desk. "How do you like the base?" he asked.

"It's okay. I miss my friends back in the States. But—but it's okay."

"Did you have a good friend there?"

"Yeah," I said. I thought of my friend Stephen. I could see him standing on the sidewalk outside my old house, waving sadly as the taxi pulled away.

"You'll have to make new friends here," said Claude.

I nodded.

"You know Cannonball, right?"

"Yeah."

"He's funny."

I smiled. "Yeah, he is."

"He kids me sometimes. But I think he likes me."

I studied Claude's face to see if he was joking. But he

wasn't. He had no idea. No idea that he was the last person Cannonball wanted to be with. "Do you have any other friends?" I asked.

Claude shook his head. "Not really. People on the base think I'm French 'cause my father is, and people in the village think I'm English 'cause my mother is. I guess I'm not exactly either."

Claude looked down at his desk. Next to the photograph of him and his father was another, smaller picture. A muscular man with fierce eyes stood on a sandy beach, arm in arm with a pretty dark-haired woman. Their bathing suits, the texture of the photograph itself, suggested a time long past. "My *grand-père* and my *grandmère*," said Claude. He looked up. "O.B., try not to talk too much about the base at dinner, okay?"

"Okay," I said, shrugging. "Why not?"

"Sometimes," said Claude, "my *grand-père* gets bothered by all the new things around here."

"Claude!" a deep voice called from the hallway.

Claude's eyes lit up. "Dinner!" he said.

11

Pop! The cork exploded from the heavy green bottle. Claude's grandfather, Monsieur LeClair, wiped the bottle top with his napkin, then held the bottle toward me. *"Voulez-vous du—"*

"Parles anglais, Grand-père," said Claude's mother, Madame LeClair. "Speak English."

Monsieur LeClair frowned. "Do you want some wine?" he asked, forcing each word from his mouth.

No one had ever asked me that before. "I—I—"

"He doesn't drink wine, *Grand-père,*" Claude interrupted.

Madame LeClair touched my arm. *"Grand-père's* ways are different from yours," she whispered.

The dining room table was set with fine china. Steam rose from blue-and-white serving dishes. On one plate, chicken and mushrooms lay in a thick white sauce. On another, butter flowed like lava down a mountain of mashed potatoes. Onions, smothered in cream, swam in a shallow bowl. Claude pushed the plate with the chicken toward me. "You first," he said.

I jabbed my fork into the dish and lifted a piece of chicken carefully onto my plate.

"Where are you from in the States?" asked Madame LeClair.

"Kind of all over," I said. "I lived in Massachusetts. Before that, in Virginia and New York, and Ohio and North Carolina."

"I have a sister in Vermont," said Madame LeClair. "Upstate, near Burlington. Have you ever been there?"

"Yeah, I went to camp near there," I said. "Just for a week." I glanced at Claude's grandfather. He was busy filling his plate. He did not look up. It was as if I were not even there.

"My mom worked in London during the last war," said Claude. "That's where she met my father."

I nodded, then shoveled a spoonful of potatoes onto my plate. I waited for someone to begin, but everyone seemed to be waiting for me. Finally, I cut a sliver of chicken and popped it into my mouth. It was tender and sweet and tasted delicious.

"There's plenty more," said Madame LeClair, "so help yourself."

Claude grinned and dug into his own plate.

The room in which we sat was tidy and clean, but everything seemed old. The walls were a faded yellow, and long thin cracks zigzagged across the ceiling. The furniture was heavy and dark. Even the paintings on the wall were of another age. In one, horses pulled a fancy carriage through a village street. In another, young girls in long white dresses joined hands in a dance. The apartment was more like a museum than a home.

"Are you enjoying France?" Madame LeClair asked.

"Yes."

"But he misses his friends," Claude added. "And he misses the United States."

"Hmmmph!" Monsieur LeClair muttered. "It's too bad more Americans do not want to go back to the United States."

I looked up, not sure I had heard Claude's grandfather correctly.

"Shhhh, *Grand-père*," Madame LeClair said, gently scolding.

"*Grand-père,*" said Claude quickly, "tell O.B. about the time I fell asleep in the organ loft."

The old man waved his hand to silence his grandson. "I'm not finished," he said. "Maybe during the war we needed help from the United States, but France can defend herself now. We don't need American soldiers, American families, here anymore."

I lowered my eyes, not sure whether I was supposed to answer.

"How can you say that, *Grand-père?*" Claude demanded. "The Americans are good for us!"

"Good for us?" Monsieur LeClair said. "How are they

good, Claude? Hmmmm? You tell me. They take our land to make their bases. They take our roads. They take everything French and try to make it American."

"But—" Claude started.

"And they're rude," Monsieur LeClair continued. "We learn their language. How many learn ours? Rude!" he said again, his color rising. "Last week when I was riding my bicycle, an American soldier yells at me, 'Get off the road, old man!' Maybe he thinks I don't understand. *I understand!* I fought for this land before he was born. This is my road! My village! And no American tells me what to do here!"

I felt my eyes stinging. I wanted to run from the room.

Madame LeClair raised her hand in the air. "*Sois tranquille, Grand-père!* I won't listen to any more of this. Whatever others have done to you is not this boy's fault. He's Claude's friend. And he's our guest."

"He is the son—" Monsieur LeClair began.

"*Grand-père*, please!" Madame LeClair said.

"He—"

"Please stop!" Madame LeClair almost shouted.

Monsieur LeClair shifted in his chair. He put both hands on the table and leaned forward as if to speak. The redness in his face began to fade. "I—I—" he stuttered. He shook his head, lifted his napkin from his lap, and dropped it onto the table. Then he pulled himself from the chair and walked slowly from the room.

There was an awkward silence. An *awful* silence. Claude sat frozen in his chair, unable to speak. I did not know what to say. "I didn't mean to cause trouble," I finally blurted.

"Oh no, O.B.," said Madame LeClair, "don't even think that." She took a deep breath. "Claude's grandfather has not been himself. He's getting older and—and things just seem to bother him now."

I nodded and looked down at my plate. I could not even think of eating. From the corner of my eye, I watched Claude stare grimly into the air.

"Would you rather come back another time?" Madame LeClair asked.

"I guess so," I said. I swung my legs from under the table and stood up.

"You don't have to go," said Claude frantically.

"No, I better," I said. "I told my mother I wouldn't stay long."

Madame LeClair walked with me to the door. "I'm so sorry, O.B.," she said quietly.

"It's okay."

"You make sure you come back, all right? I promise it will be different."

I glanced back at the table. Claude was as still as the statue in the square. He could not even bring himself to turn around. I felt bad for him. And I wished there were something I could say. But I could think of nothing. And all I wanted to do was go home.

12

The rocket blazed into the sky above the village, pulling a long white tail behind it. When it reached its peak, there was a flash and a clap, like thunder. Then all that remained was a thousand tiny embers, glowing red, drifting to the ground. "Not bad," said Cannonball. "Not as good as the Fourth of July, but not bad."

It was July 14, the day the French celebrate the capture of the Bastille prison in Paris during the French Revolution. A day of parties, fireworks, and great celebration. I stood with Cannonball on the dirt trail that ran alongside the base road. "Why don't we watch from here?" I said. "We can see pretty good."

"Nah, we can watch better in the village," said Cannonball. "Might even see them setting 'em off. C'mon." Cannonball plodded ahead like a bear on an evening stroll. I waited a moment, then followed.

I did not want to go to the village. Claude had to be there somewhere, and I could not risk seeing him. Not tonight. Not with Cannonball at my side. In the days after that awful visit, Claude seemed to have vanished into thin air. He had not appeared at the recreation fields, and he had not shown up when the Pirates lost their second ball game. Sergeant Moss had asked me if I knew where he was, and I had lied and said no. But I knew. I knew Claude was hiding in the village, too embarrassed to see me. I knew he was afraid I wouldn't talk with him. I knew he didn't know what to say. I knew exactly why Claude hadn't shown up at the ball field.

Cannonball jerked his thumb toward an old barn connected to an even older farmhouse. A pile of fresh manure between the barn and the road reeked like an open sewer. Cannonball scrunched his face and pressed his nose with his fingers. "French perfume factory!" he yelled. I smiled. I couldn't help it. But I was glad Monsieur LeClair was not there to hear.

The sleepy square was wide awake when we arrived. Near the church steps two men were shouting. "*Glace!* Ice Cream! *Glace!*" Beside them, an old woman was hawking balloons and seashells filled with a sugary candy. Cars, motorbikes, and bicycles were everywhere. There was hardly room to walk. We pushed ahead toward the crowd of villagers, soldiers, and children from the base who encircled the great bronze statue. I hopped onto a small bench and peered over the bobbing heads. The French police, the *gendarmes*, had roped off an area near the statue. Two men squatted by a rocket that was pointing toward the sky. A tiny flame flickered in one of the men's hands.

"What d'ya see!?" Cannonball bellowed.

"They're settin' one off!" I said.

There was a loud whooosh! as the missile shot into the air. It cut through the sky like a shooting star, then exploded in a dazzling yellow light.

"All riiiight!" Cannonball cried above the din.

I watched as the smoke and embers dissolved in the blackness of the night, then lowered my eyes to the crowd. I needed to know where Claude was. I had to be ready if my name was called from the shadows. But what would I say? What if Claude tried to talk to me? What if he tried to apologize? Then Cannonball would know everything—and so would everyone else.

The square was dark, but the shops and houses cast enough light so that faces could be seen. I scanned the crowd for a skinny face buried beneath a floppy beret. But Claude was nowhere to be found. I breathed a sigh of relief and stepped down from the bench.

"You see Stanton and Nick?" asked Cannonball.

"No."

"They're supposed to be coming." Cannonball grinned. "Said they might even bring a few firecrackers."

"They're allowed to do that?" I looked around to see if anyone had heard, but no one was watching us.

Cannonball gave me a playful shove. "Come on, O.B., have a little fun. It's Bastille Day. We're supposed to be celebrating. Besides," he added, "the French are gonna be plenty happy we Americans are here."

"What do you mean?"

"You know, with what's happening in Germany."

"What's happening there?" I asked.

"Don't you listen to the radio?"

"Yeah . . . sometimes." I didn't tell Cannonball that I never listened to the radio news and that I hadn't picked up a newspaper since I'd moved in. My library books had been my only reading.

Cannonball leaned his head toward me. "It's the Russians," he said solemnly. "They're at it again."

"At what?"

"You know how they kinda rule East Berlin?"

I nodded. My teacher had told us about it in school last year. After Germany lost the Second World War, it was divided into four zones. The American, French, and British zones became the country known as West Germany; the Soviet Russian zone became the country known as East Germany. The city of Berlin was located smack dab in the middle of the Soviet Russian zone. But because it was so important, the Western nations were not about to let the Russians have it. So it, too, was divided into sectors. The American, French, and British sectors became known as West Berlin. The Soviet Russian sector became known as East Berlin. My teacher had called West Berlin an island of freedom in a sea of Communism.

"Well," said Cannonball, "the Russkies want control over all of Berlin. Not just their part of the city. And they're getting really mad 'cause a lot of East Berliners are moving to West Berlin. You know, doctors, teachers, and scientists. People like that. Now—" Cannonball stopped as another rocket showered the sky with green light. "Now the soldiers and police in East Berlin are even harassing the people who cross to the West to work." His voice dropped to a loud whisper. "My dad says that if the Russians ever try to take over West Berlin, or try to cut off East Berlin so people can't leave, it'll be World War III!"

I shook my head. Why didn't I know about this? Why hadn't anyone told me? "What do you think's going to happen?" I asked.

"Dunno." Cannonball shrugged. "But if a shootin' war starts, I'll be ready."

"Yeah, right," I said.

Cannonball smiled. "You think I'm kidding? I'm not."

Another rocket exploded, turning the sky blood red. I watched as the red disintegrated in a hazy ring of smoke, and the smoke drifted off toward a thousand flickering stars. I tried to picture in my mind a map of Europe. How far away was Berlin? How long would it take a Russian missile to land in France? How long would it take a Russian tank to get here? I felt a tug at my sleeve.

"C'mon," Cannonball said, "the guys must have forgotten they were gonna meet me. Let's see if they're at the rec hall."

We turned and started to retrace our steps. Suddenly I stopped. I had a strange feeling, an eerie feeling that I was being watched. I glanced back at the statue. Everything looked the same. My eyes drifted across the square. Light filled the window in the apartment above the bakery and showed a dark form leaning at the sill. I looked at Cannonball, then back at the window. Like a phantom, the figure had disappeared.

13

Dark clouds blew in on a stiff wind that rattled the living room windows. I sank into the soft cushions of my father's favorite chair and looked outside. The sky flashed white, then fat drops began to bounce on the street like gymnasts on a trampoline. Tiny streams flowed down the driveway and puddled in shallow ponds near the curb. It was not a day for a ball game.

"You close the windows, Terry?" my mother called from the kitchen.

"Yup!"

"The one in the bathroom, too?"

"Yup!"

"Doesn't look good for this afternoon, does it?"

My mother was closer now, and I turned toward her. She was leaning against the door that led from the kitchen to the living room, her dark brown hair pulled back in a ponytail, her arms crossed on her chest.

"No," I said, "the field will never dry out."

My mother stared past me through the wavy lines of water that streaked the window. "It's pretty," she said.

"Pretty?"

"Mmmm." My mother walked to the window without moving her eyes. "The colors. They always seem so much richer in the rain. Like looking at a painting."

"It's just rain, Mom."

My mother smiled. "I suppose," she said.

I watched my mother as she watched the rain. She seemed relaxed now that all the boxes were unpacked and the footlockers were stacked neatly in the storage room. She had even begun to invite new friends to visit. Slowly, she was starting to return to her regular routines.

My mother pulled her eyes from the window. "I can't wait till we can go on vacation," she said.

"Where do you want to visit first?"

"Rome," my mother said without hesitating. "Then the Riviera," she added quickly. "And the tulip gardens in Holland."

"What about Germany?" I waited to catch my mother's reaction.

"There, too."

"You know what's happening in Berlin?" I asked.

"You mean with the Russians?"

"Yeah."

"Yes, I know."

"How come you didn't tell me?"

My mother shrugged. "I thought you knew, Terry. It's been all over the papers."

"I didn't know," I snapped.

"Well, I wouldn't worry too much about it. These things usually work themselves out."

"Cannonball says it's gonna be World War III," I blurted.

My mother shook her head. "I think Cannonball likes to exaggerate."

"But what if he's right, Mom? What if he's right this one time?"

My mother touched my shoulder. "If it gets too dangerous," she said quietly, "they'll move us to a safer place."

"Is that what Dad says?"

"Yes, that's what Dad says."

My mother raised her eyes to the window and let them linger on the rain. Then she recrossed the room. "I'm going to the chapel later," she said from the kitchen door. "Father Quinn told me he'll need some more altar boys this year. You want me to sign you up?"

I shrugged. I had not served as an altar boy at mass for half a year. "I'm getting kinda old, Mom."

"Well," my mother said, "you don't have to decide today." She turned and stepped into the kitchen.

I settled back in the chair and stretched my legs. My mother was probably right about Berlin. Cannonball could make a mountain out of any molehill. And even if a war did start, we were far enough away to get out. I closed my eyes, and my thoughts began to drift from tanks and missiles to balls and bats. In another two games, the season would be half over. Half a season, and I'd still be on the farm team. Half a season and I'd still be stuck at the scoreboard.

The tinny buzz of the doorbell startled me. I checked the window. There were no cars in front of the house. No cars across the street.

Bzzzzzz! The bell hummed angrily.

"Terry!" my mother called.

"I got it!" I grabbed the sides of the chair and pushed myself up. Who would be crazy enough to be out in weather like this? I yanked open the front door. A scarecrow of a figure stood in front of me. His legs poked like stems from his tan shorts. His red beret sagged to the side of his head like a waterlogged sponge. "Claude!" I said.

Claude took the thick towel from my mother and patted his forehead. "Dry your hair, too," my mother ordered, "or you'll be good and sick tomorrow." She lifted Claude's soggy beret from his head and pulled him out of his limp jacket. "I'll hang these in the back hall," she said.

For a moment, I could do nothing but stare. Claude looked like something that had been dragged from a swamp. His black hair was plastered flat across his brow. Droplets formed at his temples and trickled like tears down the sides of his cheeks. His skin was the color of a fish's belly. Finally I found my voice. "What are you doing here?"

"Just taking a walk," said Claude.

"Yeah, right."

Claude smiled. "Actually," he said, leaning toward me, "I came to borrow a raincoat."

I could feel a grin tugging at my lips. It had been eleven days since I'd last talked to Claude. Eleven days since I'd heard his corny jokes and silly stories. "Why'd you really come?" I asked.

"To see you."

"In the rain?"

Claude shrugged. "*Pourquoi pas?* Why not?"

"You want to go to my room?"

"Sure."

I led Claude down the hallway and pushed open the door to my room. Claude followed me inside, turning his head slowly, taking in everything. "I've never been in one of these houses," he said.

"How d'ya like it?"

"It's nice, but . . ."

"But what?"

"But it isn't over a bakery," said Claude, smiling. He pulled out the wooden chair at my desk and sat down.

"Where you been?" I asked.

Claude lowered his eyes and seemed to study his hands. "Around," he said.

"Sergeant Moss was looking for you. I did the scoreboard last game."

"I know." Claude raised his eyes. "I saw you."

"You were there?"

"I—I started to go there," Claude stammered, "but—"

Claude threw the wet towel over his shoulder, stood up, and walked to the window. For a while he just stared through the panes. I couldn't tell what he was looking at, or if he was looking at anything at all. "I'm sorry about what happened," he said at last.

"It's okay."

"It's *not* okay," said Claude. "And my *grand-père* feels bad, too." Claude took a deep breath. "This Wednesday he's taking me to Verdun. To the fort at Douaumont."

"Really?"

Claude nodded. "It's a very special place for him. And he wants you to come."

"Are you sure?"

"*Oui.* Very sure."

"I'll have to ask," I said. "But I know it'll be okay," I added quickly.

Claude beamed. *"Bon!"* he said. He glanced down at the wet clothing pasted to his skin. "I'd better go home and change."

"What time do we go?" I asked. "I mean on Wednesday."

"Eight," said Claude. "We'll meet you at eight." He walked to my bedroom door, then stopped and looked back. *"A bientôt,"* he said. "See you soon."

14

"A sacred place," Monsieur LeClair had called it on the ride
to Verdun. And he was right. It was hard to explain, but
there was an aura, a special feeling, to Douaumont. Maybe
it came from the fort itself, sunk deeply into the earth. Or
from the crumbling pillboxes and rusted cannon turrets
atop it. Maybe it came from the surrounding forests and
fields, rich and green, but still pocked and scarred by the
shells of war. Maybe it came from the tourists, walking
quietly, speaking in hushed voices, as if in a church.
Wherever the feeling came from, it was very real. You
knew that something great and terrible had once happened
here.

Monsieur LeClair leaned heavily against the handle of
his walnut cane and gazed out over a field splashed with
poppies and dandelions. Even in his dark suit he still had
the look of a warrior. His white hair, cropped close at the
sides, jutted stiffly from beneath a black beret. His skin
was taut, his jaw strong and set. The medals and red rib-

bons pinned to his coat bore witness to the courage of his youth. "There were only a handful of our soldiers here when the Germans came," the old man said. "There should have been many more. It was—how do you say—a mix-up."

I glanced at Claude. He stood transfixed at his grandfather's side, taking in every word of a story he must have heard many times before.

"It was winter," Monsieur LeClair continued. "February. *Très froid.* Very cold." He seemed almost to shiver as he said the words. "The Germans had shelled the fort, but could not break through the roof and destroy it." He tapped his cane on the ground. "But then a small group of German soldiers came—brave soldiers—and sneaked under the big guns. They walked right into the fort and captured it. It was a horrible blow for France. We had to get the fort back. And we did. It took many months—and many lives. But we did it."

Monsieur LeClair closed his eyes to see the past. He did not speak. Whatever memories, whatever horrors were etched in his mind, he would not or could not share.

"Grand-père," said Claude, squeezing the old man's arm, "will you show O.B. the place you were fighting when you were wounded?"

"No, no," said Monsieur LeClair.

"Please, *Grand-père.*"

Monsieur LeClair turned his head toward me. "O.B. does not want to hear the stories of an old man," he said.

"Please," Claude pleaded.

"I'd like to see it," I said. "If it's okay."

Monsieur LeClair hesitated. Then he looked at Claude. "All right," he said at last. He shifted his weight away from the cane and started off across the thick layer of earth that covered the roof of the fort. Claude and I followed.

"Is it close?" I whispered.

Claude nodded. "Very close."

It was an odd sensation walking across the top of the great fort. Monsieur LeClair had told us that when the fort was built, layers of concrete and sand had been placed on it to protect it from shelling. Then mountains of earth had been heaped onto the concrete. Now grass grew where the soil had been laid. It was almost like strolling through a park—a park pitted with craters and haunted by the spirits of the dead.

After three or four minutes of walking across the uneven ground, Monsieur LeClair stopped at a rusty gun turret that swelled from the earth like a metal hill. "Here," he said. "Here is where it happened." He leaned his back against the turret and clutched the top of his cane with both hands. "When the Germans pulled back, I was ordered to come here with my field glasses to do reconnaissance. A good friend, a private named Philippe, came with me." Monsieur LeClair looked down and seemed to study the ground. "It was very different then," he said. "There was no grass, and much of the earth had been blown away." He tapped the turret's thick crust with his knuckles. "We were standing right here when the Germans started to fire their artillery. You could hear the shells whistle as they came down. I dived to the ground. Right there," he said, pointing to a spot several feet away. "One of the shells must have landed nearby. I felt a terrible pain, a burning in my back and leg. I called to Philippe." Monsieur LeClair's voice began to tremble. " 'Philippe! Philippe!' But he did not answer. I crawled to him but— but there was nothing I could do." The muscles in the old man's face quivered. "Nothing," he repeated.

I had a hollow feeling in the pit of my stomach, much like the one I'd had when I held the German soldier's boot in Claude's room. A soldier, a young man, had died on this very spot. Right at my feet.

Monsieur LeClair pushed himself away from the turret. "Come," he said, "we must go."

Claude and I trailed behind as the old man retraced his steps.

"Unbelievable, isn't it?" Claude whispered.

I nodded. "Hard to see how they kept fighting for so long," I said.

Monsieur LeClair must have heard me. "You must remember, O.B.," he said, turning around, "we could have had no better reason to fight. We fought for our homes. We fought for our land. We fought for our very existence."

We continued in silence until we reached the parking lot. Tourists spilled from a bus parked near Monsieur LeClair's car. A young American soldier watched us approach. "Excuse me, sir!" he called to Monsieur LeClair. He jogged toward us. "Excuse me!" he called again.

Monsieur LeClair straightened up and waited.

The young soldier stopped an arm's length in front of us. He could not have been more than eighteen or nineteen years old and was painfully thin. His baggy shirt billowed at his waist and his cap drooped over his brow. "*Ex . . . excusez . . . ah . . .*"

"I speak English," said Monsieur LeClair.

The soldier sighed, relieved. "I—I couldn't help but notice you wearin' all those medals, sir," he said, his eyes flashing. "I was wonderin' if you were in the battle here."

"I was," said Monsieur LeClair proudly.

"Would it be all right, sir, if I took your picture?"

Monsieur LeClair put one hand on Claude's shoulder, the other on mine. "Only," he said, "if these boys can stand with me."

15

"Clear out!" Cannonball commanded. He swept his arm in front of him like a police officer directing rush hour traffic. "C'mon! Clear out!"

A group of nine-year-olds glanced up nervously at the hulking figure on the diving board. Then they began a frantic flight to the sides of the pool. When the water beneath the board was empty and still, Cannonball cupped his hands around his mouth. "Watch this, O.B.!" He took three measured steps back, closed his eyes, and drew in a long breath. Like a wild boar, he charged forward, bouncing high off the board and tucking his body in a tight ball. For a long moment, he seemed suspended in the air. Then he plunged into the water, raising a huge, drenching spray. On both sides of the pool, well beyond the safety mats, the water fell hard and heavy.

When Cannonball's head broke the water's surface, the youngsters clinging to the pool's slippery sides erupted in loud appreciation. At the base swimming pool, Cannonball Wall had no equal.

Several powerful strokes brought Cannonball to the shallow end of the pool. He pulled himself easily from the water and strutted to the beach chair at my side.

"Not bad," I said, tossing Cannonball a frayed white towel.

Cannonball snatched the towel with one hand and draped it around his neck. "Not bad? There's no one on this base who can do it like that!"

I knew Cannonball was right, but I couldn't pass up the opportunity to have some fun with him. "Yeah? You seen that new kid from Texas?"

"What kid?"

"Kid named Al. Moved into the sergeants' quarters last week. Must be six-two, two-twenty. Solid muscle." I turned away, waiting for Cannonball to take the bait.

"I don't know anyone named Al," said Cannonball testily. "Where'd you see this kid?"

"Post Exchange," I said, looking back.

"Six-two?"

"At least."

You could almost see the hair rise on Cannonball's neck. He looked like a dog whose territory had been invaded by a stray. He yanked the towel from his shoulder and slapped it hard against his thigh. "I'm gonna challenge this kid!" he said. "We'll have the biggest cannonball contest ever! You tell 'im I'll be waiting!"

"I'll—I'll tell him," I said, almost choking on my words.

Cannonball's eyes narrowed. "What's so funny?"

I shook my head, but I couldn't shake my laughter.

Cannonball watched me as I almost doubled over in my chair. "There isn't any kid named Al, is there?"

I tried to answer, but before I could utter a single word, Cannonball lunged forward and dug his arms under my back and legs. I felt my body being lifted from the chair and, a moment later, a shock of cold as the waters of the pool closed over me.

I paddled slowly across the pool, trying to salvage some dignity. Climbing the metal ladder, I reclaimed my chair. I could see Cannonball out of the corner of my eye, slathering oil on his chest and pretending to ignore me. He had propped up the back of his chair so that he could see everyone and everyone could see him. "Anything else you want me to tell Al?" I asked.

"O.B.," said Cannonball, "you're startin' to act like Clod. That's the same kind of bonehead thing he would've done."

"Nah," I said. "No way I'm like him."

"I'm not in the mood for jokes," Cannonball muttered. "I'm still sore about losing our game yesterday. We played awful."

I didn't know what to say. I wasn't expecting Cannonball to be so upset. But I knew he was right. The Pirates were just plain pitiful. They had lost three straight games.

The pool area was beginning to fill up now. There was nothing like a hot, muggy day to bring out a crowd. The trickle of swimmers leaving the locker rooms had turned into a steady stream. Entire families were parading alongside the pool toward the remaining chairs, which were pressed against the back fence. Fathers lugged heavy bags and carried thermos bottles, tucked like footballs under their arms. Mothers held toddlers whose bellies were encased in thick swimming tubes. Brothers and sisters teased and pushed.

"Hey, Cannonball."

Cannonball peered at me over the top of his sunglasses.

"You ever wish you had any brothers or sisters?"

Cannonball creased his brow. "You know Jack Miller?"

"No."

"He's in seventh grade. I went to his house once. He's got to share his room with three little brothers. They were like ants, O.B. All over the place. Taking his stuff. Breakin' it. Losin' it."

"So what are you saying?"

"What I'm sayin'," said Cannonball, "is that I like my own room." Cannonball adjusted his glasses and settled back in his chair. "What about you? You want some little rodents running around *your* room?"

I shrugged. "I don't know. Maybe, I guess." I don't know why I used the word "maybe." There were no "maybes" about it. I couldn't count the number of times I had thought about having a brother—or even a sister. Someone who could make a strange place seem familiar. Someone I could talk to and play catch with.

"You know what I really wish?" said Cannonball.

"What?"

"I wish I had a dog. A big dumb dog that would follow me everywhere."

"Why don't you ask your folks?"

"I did." Cannonball frowned. "They said we move around too much. That it wouldn't be fair to the poor dog."

As Cannonball spoke, I could see the picture on Claude's desk and hear Claude's words. The world's dumbest dog, he had called his Chaser. I thought of telling Cannonball how the dog would run in circles for so long he would drop in a heap, but I didn't. It just wasn't worth it.

"All riiiight!" Cannonball blurted. His arm shot out like the tail on a hunting dog.

I looked toward the locker room doors. The twins—the same girls Stanton and Nick were trying so hard to meet—were walking toward the pool. They almost made you blink. Each was the mirror image of the other. Their thick blond hair was cut in the same style and fell almost to their shoulders. They were tall and tanned and walked in the same easy gait. Even their bathing suits were identical, thin white stripes on a background of navy blue. And each carried a colorful beach towel in one hand and a transistor radio in the other.

"All riiiight," Cannonball repeated softly. He pushed himself up to get a better view. "O.B.," he said without looking over, "got to do me some cannonballing."

16

"O.B.!" The voice roared behind me. "Hey, O.B.!"

I let go of the heavy wooden handles on the lawn mower and glanced over my shoulder. Cannonball was stampeding like a crazed elephant across the recreation field toward my backyard. Something big had to be up. Something big enough to get Cannonball to run. He collapsed on the freshly cut grass in front of me and rolled onto his back. "You aren't gonna believe this," he said, gasping.

"Believe what?"

"Guess."

I dropped to the ground by Cannonball's side. "I give up."

"No, you gotta guess," Cannonball repeated between deep breaths.

"Oh, c'mon, Cannonball, just tell me."

Cannonball heaved himself up onto his elbows. "I'll give you a hint," he said. "Fourteen."

"Fourteen? That's the hint?"

Cannonball nodded excitedly.

Fourteen. What began with the number fourteen? What had fourteen in it? "Does it have anything to do with money?" I asked. "Like fourteen dollars?"

"Nah," said Cannonball. "Guess again."

"Is it like a measurement or something?"

Cannonball grimaced. "Well, kinda," he said. "You're gettin' close."

Close? Close to what? I wondered. I had no idea what he was talking about. I picked up a clump of cut grass and tossed it onto his shirt. "C'mon, Cannonball . . . please?"

"You're gettin' close," Cannonball said again. "That's all I'm going to tell you."

What was kind of close to a measurement? Fourteen things? Fourteen people? "Does it have anything to do with people?" I asked.

"Bingo!" Cannonball bellowed. He pulled his thick legs to his chest and leaned his sunburnt face toward me. "You can't tell anyone what I'm gonna say," Cannonball whispered. " 'Cause no one else knows."

"Okay," I agreed.

"Promise?"

"Yeah, I promise."

Cannonball glanced about like a spy ready to pass his nation's secrets. "Tom Higgins is rotatin' back to the States," he said quietly. He waited for his words to sink in.

"Tom Higgins . . . The right fielder?"

Cannonball bobbed his head. "You know what that means?"

Of course I knew what it meant. If Tom moved back to the States, there'd be only fourteen players on the roster—and room for one more. Sergeant Moss would have to take someone from the farm team. *And I was the farm team!* "When's he leaving?" I asked.

"Next week," said Cannonball. "His dad got his orders a long time ago. Tom just didn't tell anyone. He was afraid Sergeant Moss wouldn't let him play if he was only gonna be here half a season."

"You sure the coach doesn't know yet?"

"I just found out myself from Tom. And he swore me to be quiet. I think he's gonna tell the coach next game."

I wiped the sweat that beaded my brow. I could hardly believe it. In two games—or less—I'd be playing for the Meuse Pirates. Wearing a real uniform. Maybe even getting to the plate. "I need some more batting practice," I said.

"I can pitch to you," said Cannonball.

"And I'll need some fielding practice, too."

"No problem. The old Cannonball can smack you a few sizzlers." Cannonball grabbed the grass clump on his shirt and threw it back at me. "And, O.B., once you're on the team, maybe I'll be able to tell you about that club I'm in."

I rolled over onto my back and watched the gray-white clouds drift above me. It was almost too good to be true.

"You don't think Sergeant Moss will play with just fourteen guys, do you?"

"No way," said Cannonball. "He'll want to reward you for sticking it out. And besides, we've been playin' so crummy, maybe you can do us some good."

I felt my lips part in a smile.

"Just think," said Cannonball. "No more chasing down foul balls."

"No more packing all the equipment," I added.

"And best of all," said Cannonball, "no more being stuck on the scoreboard with Claude the Clod."

17

"Feels strange being out here," my father said. He tilted his foot and scraped his shoe across the hard rectangular rubber on the pitcher's mound.

I hefted a bat to my shoulder and waited as my father plucked a battered ball from the bright yellow pail by his feet, the same pail my mother used to wash the kitchen floor. I tried hard not to laugh. My father not only felt strange, he *looked* strange. No one wore olive drab army shorts, black socks, and white tennis shoes to the ball field. Not even Claude. "When's the last time you played?" I called quietly. "I mean, besides catch."

"Long time ago," my father said. "Probably in college."

"You any good?"

My father shrugged. "You ever hear of a player named Mickey Mantle?"

"Sure. Everyone's heard of him."

"I played as well as he did back then."

"You kidding?"

My father shook his head. "Course, at that time he was only about seven years old."

I forced back another laugh and waited for my father to pitch. If Cannonball was right, if Tom Higgins really was leaving, I had one week, maybe two, to get ready. And I needed more than Cannonball's help. I had told my father about it at dinner, and he had offered to pitch to me before he went to work. And if there was one thing I could always count on, it was my father keeping his word. He pulled me from my bed before my alarm went off, before the living room clock chimed six times. "Up and at 'em! Up and at 'em! Up and at 'em!" he called, like a broken record. A quick breakfast, and we were at the field.

I blinked at the mound. The day had dawned gray and misty, but already the sun was beginning to cut wide shafts through the clouds. It was a perfect time to practice—light enough so that I could see the ball, but not so bright that I would lose it in the sun.

"You ready, Terry?"

I gripped the bat tightly. "Ready," I said.

My father did not go into a windup. He lobbed the ball softly at the plate, much as Sergeant Moss had done at the tryout. I snatched the ball with my bare hand and whipped it back to the mound. "Dad, they threw harder than that on the Tiger Juniors. You're gonna have to really fire it."

"You want it faster?"

"Yeah."

My father nodded. This time he went into a windup— or something that looked like one—and let the ball loose.

It came in fast and straight. I swung and missed it by inches.

From the pail, my father dug a ball that looked as if a dog had chewed it. "Let's try another one," he said. Again he went into his windup and let the ball rip. Again I swung and missed.

"How many practices have you had?" my father asked.

"Three."

"And what does Sergeant Moss say about your hitting?"

I shrugged. "Says my timing's off. I'm swinging late."

"I think he's right, Terry. You're going to have to start your swing before the ball gets to you."

"If I do that," I said, "I'm gonna look like a clown. They'll be calling strikes on me before the ball even crosses the plate."

My father put his hands on his hips. "What I'm saying, Terry, is that you have to anticipate better. When the ball leaves my hand, you have to judge whether it's coming in fast or slow, high or low. And you only have about a second to do that."

"Just throw me another one," I said.

My father raised his left leg and hurled the ball toward the plate. It whistled past me and bounced into the back-stop. I could hear Cannonball groan, and Stanton and Nick snicker. One second. How could I figure it all out in one second?

My father kicked his toe into the mound, spraying the dirt. "Most of the pitchers in your league throw fastballs, right?"

"Yes," I mumbled.

"What I want you to do is this, Terry. If the ball looks like it's coming in straight, I want you to start your swing early. Okay?"

"Dad, if—"

"Terry," my father said impatiently, "don't argue with me. Just do it."

"Okay," I said. "Okay." I twisted my cleats in the dirt and lifted the bat off my shoulder. If I was going to look like a fool, at least no one would see me at this hour. "Ready," I said.

The next pitch came in as straight and hard as the last three. But this time I didn't wait for the ball to reach the plate. And this time I felt the shock of the bat meeting the ball. It was not a great hit, not a Cannonball smash, but it was solid and would have put me on first base.

"Good hit!" my father called as he watched the ball roll into center field.

I felt a rush of energy. It's strange how sometimes one little thing can change everything. How you feel. Even how you look at life. "Throw me another one, Dad!" I shouted.

My father dipped his hand in the bucket and threw another ball. And another. And another. We played until the sun dissolved the clouds and burned the dampness from the air. We played until my back ached and my arms throbbed from swinging. We played until the field was littered with white lumps.

As I ran to the outfield again to retrieve the balls, my

father called to me from the mound. "I've got to head back, Terry. I'm running late."

I glanced at my watch. It was past seven-thirty. We had been playing for well over an hour. "I'll bring everything home," I said.

My father pointed his mitt straight at me. "You can play this game, Terry. You know that." He turned and started to trot toward the gate in the fence.

"Dad!"

My father stopped and looked over his shoulder.

"Thanks."

18

"What in heaven's name is that?" my mother asked, pulling the teacup from her lips.

I dropped my spoon into the bowl and listened. There was a clattering in the distance that was growing louder. "Is it trash day?"

"No," my mother said.

"I'd better go check," I said. I squeezed out of the breakfast nook and hurried to the living room. I found the long cord by the front window and pulled open the drapes. My eyes widened. There, a stone's throw away, was Claude, pedaling furiously down the street on what must have been the oldest bicycle in France. His right hand clutched a rusty handlebar, his left held a blue beret to his head.

I jerked open the front door just as Claude swung onto the walkway. At the same time, my eyes darted to Cannonball's house down the street. There was no one in his front yard, no one at the windows.

"Hi!" Claude shouted.

"Shhhh!" I said, putting my fingers to my lips.

Claude rolled to a stop in front of me. "You want to go swimming?"

"Are you kidding?"

"No."

I stepped onto the walkway and pulled Claude, bike and all, to the side of my house, where it was safe to talk. "It's six-thirty," I whispered.

"I know," said Claude. "I waited almost two hours to come over."

I shook my head, unable to make sense of Claude's explanation.

"Remember on the trip back from Douaumont?" said Claude. "Remember how I asked if you wanted to go swimming sometime? And you said yes?"

I remembered. I was sitting in the car between Claude and his grandfather when he asked. What else could I say?

"Well, today's a good day," said Claude. "It's going to be hot."

My throat went dry. Stanton, Nick, Cannonball—everyone went to the base pool. I couldn't just show up with Claude at my side. "I—I don't think the pool opens till ten," I said.

"Not the *base* pool," said Claude. "A real place to swim."

"Where?"

"A little pond outside the village. 'Bout three kilometers from here."

"Do Americans go there?" I asked.

Claude shook his head. "No, they don't even know about it. Just the French. C'mon, O.B., you'll like it. And we can get there before everyone else."

I didn't know what to say. I never knew what to say when Claude ambushed me with his ideas. The thought of pedaling through the housing area with Claude clanking away beside me knotted my stomach. Maybe, just maybe, my mother could rescue me. "I'll have to ask," I said. "Stay here."

My mother was still in the kitchen, her head bent over the morning paper. "What was it?" she asked, looking up.

"Claude," I said.

"Claude?"

"Yeah, his bike sounds like a factory."

"Where is he?"

I jerked my head toward the side of the house. "Mom, he wants me to go swimming with him."

"Now?"

"Yeah. At a pond outside the village."

"Is it safe?"

"I guess so," I said. "The French go there. Do—do you think I should go?"

My mother fixed her eyes on me. "Do you want to go, Terry?"

I shrugged. "I don't know. What do you think?"

"I think it's up to you."

Up to me. That was not what I wanted to hear. "It's just that everyone thinks he's such a deuce, Mom."

"Forget what everyone else thinks," my mother said. "What do *you* want to do?"

It was hard to answer. There were some things I liked about Claude. He could be really funny. And he was smart. He was just so . . . so different. If only he weren't so different. But there was one thing I knew for sure. If I didn't go, Claude would be terribly upset. "I sorta promised him I'd go," I said. "Maybe I should just get it over with."

That was that. The decision was made.

I went to my room, pulled on my swimsuit, and grabbed a heavy towel from the linen closet. Then I sneaked out onto the patio and pushed my bike quietly to the side of the house.

"Can you go?" Claude asked.

I nodded.

"Bon!" said Claude.

We climbed onto our bikes and set off for the village. I dropped my head as low to the handlebars as I could, hoping no one would see me. When I reached the base road, I breathed a sigh of relief. We had made it out of the housing area.

"How do you like my new bike?" Claude shouted.

I looked over. It was hard to keep a straight face. The bike looked as if it were fresh from the junkyard—rusty, crooked, and muddy. "Looks great," I said.

Claude beamed. "Monsieur Boudreau found it when he was cleaning out his barn yesterday. It's an antique. Over forty years old."

I smiled. A barn. That figured.

In the village, we swung left past the church and the square and the stone farmhouses that lay on the outskirts of the town. And all the while Claude's bike rumbled and clattered like an angry tank. I was almost afraid to look back. Afraid that every shutter on every house in the village was flying open as we passed.

Finally Claude raised his hand like a scout on a wagon train and motioned for me to stop. He pointed to a dirt trail that snaked through a long meadow and disappeared into woods in the distance. Hard by the path an old tractor squatted, bent and broken. It was a perfect mark for the trail. We got off our bikes and walked them toward the path.

"You're gonna like the pond," said Claude. "I come here almost every morning. At least when it's not raining. It's my favorite place."

I nodded. "You ever go to the base pool?" I asked.

"Not so much."

"How come?"

Claude shrugged. "I don't know."

"Do they let you in?"

"Oh yeah, but—"

"But what?"

Claude hesitated. "But last year sometimes they used to throw me in the water."

"You mean Stanton and the guys on the team?"

"Yeah," said Claude, lowering his eyes.

"But they throw everyone in."

"Yeah," said Claude again. "But not ten times."

The long grass beside the trail slapped at our legs as we walked on. The sun was higher now, and I could feel its heat on my face and neck. Claude was right. It would be a good day to swim.

When the meadow met the woods, the trail narrowed, forcing us to leave our bikes and walk single file. Claude pushed ahead. I followed closely behind. The woods were quiet, almost graveyard quiet. There were no voices, and we had long since left behind the sounds of cars and homes. The only noises that could be heard were the rustling of leaves in the breeze and the songs of the summer birds.

Suddenly I felt something hard beneath my foot. I glanced down. A dead branch poked from under my shoe. I kicked it away, but then stopped in my tracks. I remembered my father's map, marked in black, stretched across his desk. Were the woods within the restricted area? What if that branch had been a grenade or an artillery shell? My heart began to pound. "Claude!" I yelled. "Was there fighting here during the war?"

Claude turned, startled. "No," he said, "not here." Then, maybe because he read my face, he added, "Don't worry, O.B., it's safe to walk."

We pushed ahead for several more minutes, until we came to a thread of flowing water too small to call a brook or a creek. Beyond the water, the trail split: a dirt path meandered to the left, a path of matted green growth led to the right. Claude leaped over the tiny stream, landing with a thud on the far side of its muddy bank. "We go this way," he said, nodding toward the dirt path. "The other trail goes all the way to the hill." We continued until we arrived at a small sunlit rise in the path. Claude stopped when we reached the top. "Nice, huh?" he said.

"Yeah," I agreed. A long field blanketed with white and yellow wildflowers stretched before us. Farther on, the blue waters of the pond sparkled like an enormous jewel set in the earth.

Claude let his shirt fall to the ground and raced forward. Then he took a running leap and jumped into the water, raising a huge white spray. "It's great!" he shouted. "C'mon!"

I threw down my towel and pulled off my shirt as I ran to the water's edge. "Is it deep?" I called.

"Not too," said Claude.

I stepped in and splashed the cold water on my chest and shoulders. The muddy bottom sucked at my feet as I waded forward. "It's freezing," I said.

"Just dive in," said Claude.

"It's freezing," I repeated.

"Monsieur Poulet!" Claude teased. "Mr. Chicken!"

I smiled. If Claude could do it, so could I. I bent my knees, gritted my teeth, and let the cool water envelop my chest and head. When I broke the surface, I shook myself like a dog emerging from the ocean.

Claude grinned and swam toward me. "You're going to the game Saturday, right?"

"Sure."

"Good!" Claude took a deep breath and disappeared beneath the surface. A heartbeat later, he came up behind me, spitting a long stream of water. "Until you came," he said, "I never realized how boring it was working the scoreboard alone."

"Yeah," I said. I felt a pang of guilt. Claude knew nothing about Tom Higgins moving. Nothing about the extra place on the roster.

Claude cupped his hand and splashed water in my face. "C'mon," he said. "I'll race you to the other side." He took off, his thin arms flailing, his feet thrashing.

I pushed myself off the bottom and kicked forward. Maybe later I'd tell Claude about Tom Higgins. Right now I wanted nothing more than to beat him in our first race.

19

Sergeant Moss jogged toward the on-deck circle, smiling broadly. "Got some good news," he said.

I pressed the snaps on the equipment bag and stood up. "For me?" I asked, pretending not to know.

The coach stopped and crossed his massive arms. "Yes, for you. Tom Higgins just told me he's rotating back to the States. Means we got an extra spot. *Your* spot."

I'm not sure why, but my hands started to tremble. It must have been the way the coach said it—*my* spot. It was official now. I was a Meuse Pirate. "That's great," I said. "Fantastic!"

"O.B., we're having a tough season. We can sure use your help."

"Yes, sir."

"Coach," Sergeant Moss replied. "Just Coach."

"Yes, Coach."

"Tom'll play his last game today. Then he'll drop his uniform off at your house after the game." Sergeant Moss stepped back and sized me with his eyes. "He wears an extra-large. That okay?"

"Sure," I said quickly. "That's just my size."

Sergeant Moss laughed.

"Well, you be suited up for Thursday. Six sharp."

"Yes, sir—Coach."

Sergeant Moss pointed to right field. "Better get to the scoreboard. Your buddy's waiting."

My eyes flashed to the board. Claude was sitting on the platform, his legs dangling like poles. He was watching us closely. "What about foul balls?" I asked.

"Don't worry," said the sergeant. "I got another boy to chase them down."

I gave my hat a tug and took off toward the fence. My buddy, Sergeant Moss had called Claude. Was that what everyone thought? I climbed the fence and lifted myself onto the platform.

"What'd the coach want?" Claude asked.

"What?"

"The coach. He want us to add a couple extra runs to the score?"

I shook my head. "Nah."

Claude eyed me suspiciously. "Must've wanted something. You were talking for a while."

I could not bring myself to answer. I looked down to escape Claude's gaze and pulled a piece of chalk from the bucket.

"C'mon, O.B.," Claude pressed. "Tell me."

"We were just talking," I said.

"Yeah."

"And . . ."

"And what?"

I had to tell Claude. I did not want to hurt his feelings, but he was sure to find out after the game. "You know Tom Higgins?"

"Course."

"He's going back to the States." I didn't need to say more.

Claude hunched his thin shoulders and looked down at his sandals. "That's good," he said quietly. *"Très bon."*

"Yeah," I mumbled.

"When are you going to start playing?"

"Thursday."

Claude pressed his lips in a tight smile and nodded.

The bleachers swelled with applause as the Pirates swarmed onto the field. Tom Higgins raced toward us, his uniform billowing even on his bulky frame. He stopped midway in right field and waved. "Thursday, O.B.!" he shouted. "Good luck!"

I tried to smile, but I couldn't. I should have been leaping from the platform with excitement, but I wasn't.

"Maybe you'll play right field, too," said Claude.

I shook my head. "No way. There are a lot of better players. I'll just sit on the bench."

"No," said Claude. "You're a good player, too. You got a good hit at practice on Wednesday."

"Just lucky," I said.

"Well, if you do get in," Claude added, "I hope it's in right field. Then we can talk."

"We can talk anytime," I said. "We can still see each other. It's not like I'm moving or something."

"No," said Claude, "not like that. But it'll be different."

We settled back in silence and watched the game play out. It went just the way the last game did. Stanton and Nick reached first and second base, but nobody could bat them in. Even Cannonball couldn't keep his towering fly balls in fair territory. The team was in a slump. A miserable slump. When the sixth inning ended, I added the numbers Claude and I had chalked on the board. Metz Marauders—3, Meuse Pirates—0. Another game. Another loss. Sergeant Moss would not be happy.

Claude threw his chalk in the bucket and slid off the platform. "They're playing terrible," he said.

"Yeah."

"You—you want to come to my house?" Claude asked.

"Can't," I said. "Gotta get home. Tom's going to drop his uniform off."

Claude nodded. "Maybe I'll see you Thursday." He turned and walked slowly toward the village, his eyes locked on the ground.

"Claude!" I called.

Claude stopped, but he did not turn.

"You want to go swimming tomorrow?"

Claude wheeled around. "The pond?"

I could almost hear the life flow back into his voice. "Yeah," I said.

Claude cocked his head as if he were thinking it over. Then he said, "On one condition."

"What?"

"You come to my music recital the week after next."

"You got a deal," I said. *"A bientôt!"*

Claude smiled. "When you're going to meet someone for sure the next day, you say, '*A demain!*' Means 'Till tomorrow!' "

"Okay," I said. *"A demain!"*

20

The barber's eyes gleamed as he surveyed Cannonball's huge head. "You want ah shavv?" he asked in a voice thick with accent.

Cannonball eyed the man warily. "What?"

"Shavv."

"No," said Cannonball. "No shave. I want a haircut." He looked at me and rolled his eyes.

"I think he means do you want your head shaved," I said.

"Oh." Cannonball studied himself in the long mirror at the base barbershop. "Yeah," he said after a moment. "Shave it on the top and sides, but leave a little bit sticking up in front." He patted the tuft of hair above his forehead, apparently to let the barber know where the front was.

"*Bon,*" said the barber. He pushed Cannonball's head forward, and the electric clippers whirred.

I lifted a magazine from the table and began to leaf through it. There was a full-page picture of Mickey Mantle and Roger Maris of the New York Yankees. Both were chasing Babe Ruth's record of sixty home runs in a single season. I had a quarter bet riding on it with Cannonball. He said no one could beat the Babe. I put my money on Mickey. And there was a story on South Vietnam. President Kennedy was afraid that the Communists would take it over and that all Southeast Asia would fall to them. He had already sent military advisers there, and the article said he might be sending more soldiers to help out.

But the biggest article was about Berlin. Things were really starting to heat up. Almost fifteen hundred people a day were fleeing the Communist part of the city. It didn't make the Russians look so good, and Premier Khrushchev of the Soviet Union was madder than a hornet about it, and about his not having control of all of Berlin. He said if a war ever broke out, the Soviets could destroy Britain with six hydrogen bombs and could flatten France with nine more. But President Kennedy was not backing down. He warned the Russians that any attack on West Berlin would be considered an attack on the United States, and that force would be met with force. I shuddered.

"O.B.," Cannonball said, "how do I look?"

I glanced up from the news magazine. The barber had left virtually no hair on Cannonball's head. He looked like a full moon with eyes. "You look great."

"You think he took off too much?"

"No, it's perfect."

Cannonball looked in the mirror and turned his head from side to side. "Yeah," he said at last, "I look good."

"Is okay?" the barber asked.

"Yup," said Cannonball happily.

The barber sprinkled water on Cannonball's scalp and rubbed it in. Then he whipped off the sheet, sending a blizzard of blond hair through the air. As Cannonball stepped down from the chair, I stepped up. "Make mine a little longer, please," I whispered.

The barber smiled. "For you, good cut."

After my hair was clipped short enough to pass my father's inspection, Cannonball and I stepped onto the sidewalk. A fine mist filled the morning air, and we stood for a moment under the shop's red-and-white canopy.

"What do you want to do?" Cannonball asked.

"I don't know. Want to go to the library?"

You'd have thought I had asked Cannonball to kiss a lizard. His face contorted in a mask of disapproval. "It's— it's summer," he stammered. "Nobody goes to the library in the summer." He grabbed my arm and pulled me across the street. "Jeez, O.B., sometimes you talk like you're nuts."

"All right," I said. "Where do you want to go?"

"Snack bar."

"Gee, we haven't been *there* in almost two days," I said.

"I know," said Cannonball. "That's why we should go now." He turned to his right and began to plod up the street.

I fell into step. We passed the commissary and a cluster of low wooden buildings, each bearing a large sign warning that trespassers would be arrested. Across the street was the green headquarters building where my father worked. I counted the windows on the top floor. One. Two. Three. Four. Fourth from the left. That was his office. I could picture him bent over his desk—preparing for whatever Berlin might bring.

"O.B.," said Cannonball.

"Yeah."

"Some of the guys say they saw you riding bikes with Clod down the base road. I'm not saying it, but that's what they say."

My face flushed hot. "That right?"

Cannonball bobbed his head. "Yeah. Is it true?"

I shrugged. "I guess so."

"What were you doing with him?"

I hesitated. I didn't know how much Cannonball knew. How much the guys knew. Had they followed us to the pond? "You know . . . just riding around."

Cannonball shook his head. "O.B., nobody hangs around with him."

"I wasn't hanging around with him," I said. "He just asked if I wanted to go riding."

Cannonball stopped short. "Look," he said, "Clod's weird. He wears hats when it's ninety-five degrees out. He wears tiny short shorts like a girl. He wears stupid gladiator shoes."

I didn't answer.

"You know what he did to Stanton last year?" Cannonball asked, his voice rising.

"No."

"Stanton went to the village to get a chicken for his mother. The guy at the butcher shop couldn't understand him, so Stanton sees Clod in the square. He goes outside and says, 'Hey, Clod, how do I tell that guy I want a fresh chicken?' So Clod tells him to say, *'Je suis un grand poulet.'* Then he takes off like a shot. So Stanton goes back in the store and says it, and the guy starts laughing." Cannonball grimaced. "You know what *'Je suis un grand poulet'* means?"

I shook my head, but I could have guessed.

"It means 'I'm a big chicken,' " said Cannonball, almost spitting the words.

I bit my lip to keep from laughing.

"Stanton wanted to smack 'im, but he couldn't find him."

"Good thing," I said.

"Look, O.B.," said Cannonball, lowering his voice, "you're on the team now, so you gotta start acting more . . . more American. Okay?"

"Yeah," I said. "Okay."

21

"Oh and four," said **Sergeant Moss,** shaking his head. "That's the worst record of any team I've ever coached. Worst record in the base league. You boys are better than that. But you're sure not showing it." He tapped the paper in his hand. "Starting today, there're going to be changes in this lineup."

I rubbed my palms against the soft wool of my pants. Changes. They wouldn't affect me. I was happy just to be sitting in the dugout, swimming in Tom Higgins's extra-large uniform.

"Wonder what kind of changes," Cannonball whispered nervously.

"Listen up," Sergeant Moss ordered. "Carter, second. Stemmer, first." As Stemmer's name was called, Luis Garcia groaned. He had been at first all season. Now he was out of a job. "Rettig, third," Sergeant Moss continued. "Lucci, center. Anderson, short." Another boy, not Anderson, grumbled at the far side of the bench. "Wall, catcher."

Cannonball let out a huge breath, like a balloon losing its air. "Rosenthal, left. DePrado, pitcher. O'Brien, right."

O'Brien? My eyes met the sergeant's. "You heard me, O.B.," he said. "Maybe you can light a fire under this team."

Cannonball's hand slammed against my back. "All riiiight!" he whooped.

It happened so quickly I didn't have time to think, time to worry. I grabbed my mitt and scrambled after the others as they poured from the dugout. Right field seemed like a hundred miles away, and I ran to it as if chasing a mirage. My heart was pounding so hard I could barely focus on the scoreboard . . . could barely feel the hard ground beneath my feet. When I reached the fence, I stopped and stared dumbly at Claude.

"O.B., what are you doing here?"

I shook my head, not sure myself.

"You playing?"

I nodded.

"I told you," said Claude, almost bursting. "I told you you were good enough."

"Coach wants me to light a fire under the team," I finally managed to say.

"You're gonna need a torch," said Claude, smiling. Then he looked beyond me and said, "You better get ready. Game's starting."

I turned to face the infield. A short husky boy wearing the uniform of the Toul Raiders was strutting to the plate.

He held his bat like a club in his right hand. I sighed, relieved. A righty. Unless he swung late, he was almost certain to hit the ball to left or center field. I was safe—for now.

Charlie DePrado looked in from the mound and took his sign from Cannonball. Then he went into his motion and let loose a stinging fastball. "Strrrike one!" the umpire called. That strike was followed by another and another. One batter down, seventeen more to go.

After three slow innings in right field, my turn came at the plate. Fred Rosenthal had led off with a sharp single to center, our first hit of the game. Charlie DePrado moved him to second with a weak ground ball to the mound. We had a runner in scoring position. Now it was up to me.

I dug my cleats into the hard dirt beside the plate and hefted my bat to my shoulder. I could see my teammates across the diamond, perched anxiously on the dugout steps. I could see my mother sitting in the front row of the bleachers, her hands pressed together as if in prayer. Concentrate. I had to concentrate. I had to put everyone and everything out of my mind. I turned my head toward the mound. From now on, it would be the pitcher, the ball, and me.

"Nice shirt," said the Raiders' catcher. "You get it from King Kong?"

I tried to ignore him, but it was hard to ignore my uniform. My shirt sleeves flapped like an elephant's ears. My pants could have hidden a small family.

"Maybe you could make a parachute out of it," the catcher teased. "Or a sail."

I stepped out of the box and sucked in a deep breath. I knew what the catcher was up to. But I wasn't going to let him bother me. I stepped back to the plate and held my bat so tightly I could feel the blood pulsing in my hands. The noise was building like an oncoming train. Cheers from the stands. Cheers from the dugout. I could even see Claude standing on the scoreboard platform, his hands cupped to his mouth.

The pitcher was a tall skinny boy whose face was marked with red blotches. He stared in, glowering, but I stared right back. I couldn't show any weakness. Not now. The skinny boy leaned forward for his signal, then kicked his left leg high in the air as he went into his windup. The first pitch blurred into the catcher's mitt. "Strrrike one!" the umpire shouted.

I glanced at the dugout. "You can do it, O.B.!" Sergeant Moss called. "Watch the ball! Watch the ball!" My eyes shifted back to the mound. The skinny boy was nodding at the catcher's sign. A fastball. Somehow I knew his second pitch would be a fastball. He had beaten me the first time with one. He would try it again. I started into my swing a moment after the ball left the pitcher's hand, just as my father had taught me. It streaked like a missile toward me, but my bat was already over the plate.

Crack! The ball rocketed off the wood and soared high and deep into left field. It bounced once, then rolled to a stop at the fence. For an instant, I couldn't move. I couldn't take my eyes off the tiny white lump nestled like an egg against the chain link. I had never hit a ball so hard, so far. Sergeant Moss's voice brought me back to the game. "Run!" he roared. "Run!"

I took off like a scared rabbit. I touched first and scrambled toward second. As I made my turn, the third-base coach held his arms high in the air, the signal to stop. I pulled up on the second-base bag and looked back at the batter's box. Fred Rosenthal was bouncing triumphantly across the plate. The bleachers erupted and the players began to leap in the dugout like monkeys in a cage. I turned to the scoreboard. Claude was dancing a frenzied jig as he chalked in the run—Pirates—1, Raiders—0. I could not pull my eyes from the huge "1"—my "1."

We took to the field three more times. And three more times we kept the Raiders from scoring. Then it was over. I jogged back, almost floated back, to the dugout. We had done it. I had done it. I had made a difference. I had finally proved I belonged.

As I neared the first-base line, the team rioted around me. I felt my legs being lifted from the ground, and a second later I was bobbing on Cannonball's shoulders above a sea of blue hats. A hand grabbed my arm. "O.B.!" a voice shouted.

I looked down. Stanton was standing beside me, a wild grin on his face. "We're going to the snack bar!" he yelled. "You want to come?"

I glanced back at the scoreboard. Claude was standing behind the fence, his arms resting on the metal crossbar, watching me.

"You coming?" Stanton called again.

"Yeah," I said. "I'm coming."

22

My mother lifted the white shirt from the ironing board and held it up. "This looks fine," she said, passing it to me. "What pants are you going to wear?"

"The brown ones," I said.

My mother furrowed her brow. "I think your gray pants would look nice, too."

"All right," I said. Brown pants. Gray pants. It didn't matter. No one from the base was going to see me.

"What time does it start?" my mother asked.

"Eight."

"Are a lot of people going?"

"Don't think so. Just some people from the village."

"Imagine having your own concert," my mother said. "Claude must be very proud."

"He is," I said. I draped the shirt over my arm and went to my room. It was hard to explain, hard to admit, but I was looking forward to going. It wasn't that I was crazy about church music, there was just something exciting about hearing Claude play for the first time. I wanted him to do well. I wanted people to like him. I was nervous for him. Claude was nervous for a different reason. He was so afraid no one would show up he had made me promise three times I'd be there.

When I finished dressing, I said my goodbye and walked onto the patio. My bike was waiting, but I decided not to ride it. No sense calling attention to myself. It would be better to walk. I struck out across my backyard toward the recreation field. Except for a few children on the swings, it was deserted. There would be no witnesses tonight.

The evening was as pretty as the day had been. The sun had turned a fiery orange and was throwing streaks of red, purple, and pink across the sky. Dark shadows pulled from the trees, hiding the wildflowers that grew in clusters along the base road. The air was still, the birds quiet. I set my sights on the thin spire above the village. It was like a compass, guiding me, drawing me to the church.

The square was bustling when I arrived. Cars, bicycles, even a new tractor were packed onto the side roads. Old couples hobbled forward, leaning on their canes. Children dashed along the sidewalks in front of their mothers. Men in dark blue suits walked in knots, smoking cigarettes and talking quietly. They had all come to hear Claude.

I stood near the worn steps of the church. The huge wooden doors had been pulled open, and a warm light shone inside. I decided to wait until the other guests had entered. Then I would slip in and sit in the back.

"O.B.!" a voice hollered.

I jerked my head so quickly the muscles snapped in my neck.

"Over here!"

My eyes followed the voice and found the speaker. My chest tightened. There, sprawled beneath the bronze statue, were Cannonball and Nick, munching on long loaves of bread. Cannonball was motioning frantically for me to join them. I left the steps and jogged over.

"What are you doing here?" Cannonball thundered.

My mind raced, searching for an excuse. "My mom sent me to get some bread."

"*Boulangerie*'s closed," said Nick. "We were the last ones in." He eyed me suspiciously. "How come you're dressed up?"

"I'm not dressed up. My mother's just washing a lot—"

"You aren't gonna believe what's happening here," said Cannonball, interrupting. "You know who everyone's coming to see?"

"No," I lied.

"Guess."

"Come on, Cannonball."

"Just tell him," Nick ordered.

"Clod," said Cannonball, almost choking on the name.

"Claude?" I asked. "How come?"

Nick jabbed his finger at a poster tacked to a telephone pole near the street. Claude's face, in black and white, stared out onto the square. Above the picture, the words CONCERT DE MUSIQUE RELIGIEUSE were printed in bold black letters.

"Looks like something at the post office," said Cannonball. "Wanted. Claude the Clod. For being the world's biggest deuce. Five feet seven inches tall. Thirty-one pounds. Do not attempt— Do not attempt—" Cannonball's words were lost in his laughter.

"He's doing a concert?" I asked Nick.

Nick nodded. "Didn't he tell you? Thought you guys were friends."

"No," I said. "He didn't tell me."

Cannonball rolled onto his side, clutching his stomach. "Do—do not attempt to capture him," he gasped. "He's armed with a deadly beret."

I tried not to pay attention to Cannonball, but it was hard to ignore a whale thrashing at my feet.

Nick patted the ground beside him. "Sit down," he said.

I dropped to the grass and glanced at my watch. Almost eight. Not much time to get inside. I watched the last of the villagers file into the church. Then two men pulled the massive doors closed. My stomach churned. "He must be pretty good," I said.

"Yeah," said Nick.

"You guys want to go in and listen?"

Nick frowned. "What, are you kidding?"

"Yeah," I said. "Just kidding."

There was a swell of applause. Then the first strains of music filled the church and filtered into the square. I closed my eyes. It was almost like listening to a record. The music rose and fell in waves of seamless beauty. I could picture Claude, sitting in the organ loft, his long fingers racing across the keys. Lost in his music. Lost in his own world. Did he know I wasn't there?

Cannonball pushed himself up from the ground, still giggling. He caught his breath and cupped his hands to his mouth. "Play 'Take Me Out to the Ball Game'!" he shouted in a voice that could be heard in Paris. Then he dissolved again in laughter.

"Shut up, Cannonball," I blurted. I stared at the heavy doors guarding the church. It was too late now. I had broken my promise. I had let Claude down.

23

Claude's face haunted my thoughts that night and kept sleep away. I could see him, looking down from his seat at the organ, searching for me. I could see the disappointment in his eyes as he scanned one row of chairs after another. I wanted to tell him that I *was* there. Not in the church, but close by. I wanted him to know that I had listened to his music and that I had heard the church shake with applause when he had finished. I wanted him to know that I had not forgotten.

I rolled onto my side and stared at the clock. Five-thirty. I pushed myself up, leaned forward, and drew back the curtain on my window. The moon hung over the village like a shiny white button, but already there were signs of life. A rooster crowed in the distance, and an old tractor coughed and rumbled. Here and there, tiny beads of light marked the homes of farmers and shopkeepers preparing for the new day. The *boulangerie* would open soon, and Claude would be there. So would I.

. . .

The baker, Monsieur Girard, glanced over his shoulder when the bells jingled on the door. *"Bonjour,"* he said cheerily. *"Attendez un instant."* His arms were filled with fresh *baguettes*, the thin crusty loaves I had come to like so much. The old man placed them carefully in a wide basket. Then he wiped his hands on his apron and leaned against the counter. *"Comment ça va?"* he asked.

"Ça va bien, merci," I replied. The words came quickly. Claude would have been proud. *"Je voudrais du pain,"* I added.

The old man laughed and gestured at the bread heaped in the baskets around us. *"J'ai beaucoup de pain. Qu'est-ce que vous voulez?"* He paused. "What do you like?"

I bent over a basket and pretended to inspect a fat round loaf.

The old man watched me for a moment, then held his finger in the air, signaling for me to wait. *"Attendez ici,"* he said, vanishing into the back room. He returned carrying a tray filled with steaming brown croissants.

I fumbled in my pocket for change. *"Com—combien?"* I asked.

"Rien," said the old man. "You take." He held the tray in front of me. *"Ils sont chauds,"* he warned. "Hot."

"Merci," I said. I lifted one of the flaky quarter moons and bit off the tip. The buttery bread melted on my tongue.

"Est-ce bon?" the old man asked.

"Oui," I said. *"Très bon."*

The old man smiled and nodded.

I peeked at my watch. Ten past six. Still no sign of Claude. I could not wait in the bakery all morning for him. And it was too early to knock on his door. It would be best to sit by the statue and wait. *"Au revoir,"* I said.

"A bientôt," the old man replied.

The bells jingled again when I pulled open the door to the bakery. I fixed my eyes on the bronze soldier. He was becoming a friend, and I found comfort in his presence. I stepped onto the sidewalk and down to the street to be near him.

"Why are you here?" a voice demanded.

I spun around. Claude was standing in the shadows of the entryway that led up to his apartment.

"Hi," I said.

"Why are you here?" Claude repeated. His voice left no doubt that he knew I had broken my promise.

"Come to see you," I said.

"I don't have anything to say to you," said Claude. He took the doorknob in his hand and twisted it.

"Please, Claude. Just listen."

Claude stared coldly at me, but he did not leave.

"I just wanted to say, you know—" The apology I had prepared on the walk to the village jumbled in my mind. "You know, that I'm sorry." I pointed quickly to the statue of the charging soldier. "I was right there. I—I just didn't go in."

"Why not?" Claude demanded.

I shrugged.

Claude's cheeks turned apple red. "My *grand-père* saw you with some of the guys, rolling around on the ground, laughing. You remember now?"

"That was Cannonball," I protested meekly. "He was the one who—"

"I know why you didn't go in," said Claude, his voice rising. "You were afraid of what they'd say. You were scared they wouldn't be your friends. You didn't want anyone to know you'd come to see Claude the Clod play his concert."

I stared at my feet, unable to speak, unable to look Claude in the eye.

"I hear what people call me," said Claude. "But I thought you were different. I thought you were better."

Claude's words ripped through me.

"Look at me, O.B. Look at me!"

I slowly raised my eyes.

"You know me better than anyone at the base. We've hung around together. We've done things together." Claude's voice began to tremble. "But you're so afraid of what people will say. You let them do your thinking for you."

"I'm sorry," I mumbled. "I just wanted you to know that—"

Claude pushed his door open and turned his back to me. "I don't want to talk to you," he said. "Not until you're ready to be my friend." He disappeared into the shadows and closed the door behind him.

24

There was a loud rapping on the front door, then, a minute later, the sound of hushed voices in the living room. I sat up in my bed. It was the middle of the night, not a time for visitors. Something terrible must have happened. I swung my legs to the floor and crept down the darkened hallway. "When?" I heard my father ask.

"Since about zero two hundred," a voice responded.

I peeked around the corner into the living room. My father was at the doorway, clutching his bathrobe at his waist. In front of him, a grim-faced captain was standing stiffly. A pistol dangled from his hip.

"Is the base on alert?" my father asked.

"Yes, sir."

"Good. Notify the staff to meet me at zero five hundred in my office."

"Yes, sir."

"And, Bob—"

"Sir?"

"Let's keep this quiet until the intelligence is all in. No sense alarming the civilians."

"Yes, sir," said the captain. He brought his hand to his brow in a crisp salute, then jogged back to a Jeep waiting on the street.

I felt an arm brush my shoulder. My mother. I had not even known she was there. "What is it, Dan?" she asked my father.

My father pushed the door closed and forced a smile. "It's nothing."

"Duty officers don't come at four-thirty in the morning for nothing," my mother said. "What's happened?"

My father's eyes darted from my mother to me. He hesitated. Then he said, "A situation has developed in Berlin."

"What kind of situation?" my mother asked.

My father dug his hands into the pockets of his robe. "The East Germans seem to be sealing off their part of the city. The base has been put on alert. I can't say any more now. There should be an announcement on the radio."

My mother's face blanched. She started to speak but stopped, as if the words had caught in her throat. My father stepped forward and kissed her gently on the forehead. Then he tousled my hair with his hand. "I have to go," he said.

After my father had gone, I pulled two chairs to the radio cabinet and tuned in the Armed Forces station. Band music swelled from the speaker.

"Why don't you go back to bed, Terry," my mother said. "I'll call you when it comes on."

"I'll wait," I said. I sank into the cushions and closed my eyes. Images ran together in my mind. Roaring tanks. Flashing cannons. Blackened cities. Was this it? Was this the beginning of the war Cannonball had talked about? What would happen to us now? What would we do? Where would we go? My mother must have sensed my thoughts. Her hand touched my arm. "Everything will be fine," she said.

I nodded, but I could tell that she did not believe her own words.

We sat in silence, listening to the music, waiting for the news we knew would come. We did not have to wait long. "We interrupt this broadcast," the announcer said, "for a special Armed Forces bulletin. During the early morning hours today, East German soldiers and police, supported by Russian-made tanks, closed the border between East and West Berlin to block the escape of refugees to the West. Barbed wire and barricades have been placed at all crossings and intersections, which are now guarded by heavily armed East German troops. It is reported that Soviet army divisions are converging on the city to prevent interference from the West. There has been no statement yet from the White House. This has been a special news bulletin. Please stay tuned for further developments."

The music returned as if nothing had happened, as if

nothing were wrong. I stared at the radio, almost expecting it to say more. "Does this mean war?" I said at last.

My mother shook her head. "No, Terry, it's just—"

There was a hard knock at the door. I jumped from my chair. Maybe my father had come back. Maybe he could tell us what was really happening. I yanked open the door and was met by a meaty face flushed red with excitement. "C'mon out," said Cannonball.

"Who is it?" my mother called.

"Just Cannonball, Mom. I'm going out front for a minute."

Cannonball pulled me onto the walkway, and we huddled together in the first light of morning. "Did they come for your dad?" he asked excitedly.

"Yeah."

"Mine, too." Cannonball looked around. When he was sure no one could hear us, he said, "My dad says this could be it."

"Really?"

Cannonball bobbed his head. "A lotta people living in East Berlin don't want to be stuck there forever under the Commies. If the East Berliners start to revolt, my dad says the Americans are gonna have to support 'em. But the Russkies won't let us. So it will be us against the Russkies."

For once in his life, Cannonball made sense. The U.S. Army was in Europe to keep peace and to make sure the Communists kept their distance. If the Russians wouldn't let people be free, President Kennedy would have to do something. "Do *you* think there's going to be a war?" I asked.

"Yup," said Cannonball solemnly. "But like I been telling you, I'll be ready."

"How?"

"That's what I came to talk to you about," Cannonball whispered. "You know the club I'm in?"

"Yeah."

"Stanton just came by. I talked with him through my window. Club's gonna have a meeting this morning. And we want you to come."

"Me?"

"Yeah. You're the only new person we're asking."

"What kind of meeting?"

"Secret," said Cannonball. "You coming?"

"I guess so. Yeah."

Cannonball smiled. "You know the bombed-out pillbox in the pasture by the base road?"

"Sure."

"Be there at eleven."

25

The pillbox had once sheltered a machine gun and its crew. Sometime during the First World War, a heavy shell must have scored a direct hit on it, atomizing its roof and leaving only the jagged skeleton of its concrete foundation. Over the years, nature had done its best to hide what was left of the tiny fortification. The winds had blown soil and seeds onto its floor, and tall grass and wildflowers now grew where soldiers had once crouched. The walls, or what was left of them, stood no higher than three feet and were matted with thick green moss. Nature had done its work well. From a distance, the pillbox was just a small lump in the earth.

I crossed the base road and stopped at the fence that surrounded the field where the pillbox lay. Four thin strands of barbed wire blocked my way. I stepped hard on the bottom wire, pushing it down several inches. Then I bent over and squeezed through the narrow opening. Several yards to my left, a black-and-white cow eyed me warily. I made a low humming sound that seemed to put her at ease, for a moment later she lowered her head and began to nibble on a small plant.

I picked my way across the pasture, stepping carefully around the fat brown droppings left by the cows and trying my best to keep the dry grass from crunching too loudly beneath my feet. A secret meeting, Cannonball had called it. I was not about to spoil that. As I approached the pillbox, I heard the murmur of voices. Then Stanton, Nick, and Cannonball came into view. They were sitting in the ruins, their backs pressed against the foundation walls, their legs stretched out in front of them.

"O.B.!" Cannonball shouted.

"Keep it down," Stanton snapped. "You want to tell the whole base we're here?"

Cannonball hung his head like a scolded dog.

Stanton motioned to a spot on the ground near his feet. "Sit down," he said, more an order than an invitation.

I dropped to the grass and crossed my legs.

Stanton leaned forward. "You know all about Berlin, right?"

I nodded.

"There might be a war," said Stanton, his voice barely rising above a whisper. "A big one."

"I know."

Stanton glanced at Nick and back at me. "If there is, we're gonna be right smack in the middle of it. There are

American bases all over France. If fighting starts, the Russians aren't going to stop in Berlin. They're gonna come right down here. Right for us."

I felt the skin tingle on the back of my neck. It wasn't that Stanton had said something I didn't know, it was the way he had put it. Right for us. If a war started, the Russians knew exactly where we were, and they'd try to smash us. Maybe with missiles, maybe with tanks. It was like sitting in the middle of a bull's-eye.

"The way I see it," Stanton continued, "if fighting breaks out, there won't be time to evacuate us, and there just aren't enough American soldiers to hold the Russians back." Nick and Cannonball nodded in agreement. "So," said Stanton, "we're gonna have to take to the woods to protect ourselves."

"Like the guerrillas in World War II," said Nick excitedly.

"And the French Resistance," Cannonball added.

"O.B.," said Stanton gravely, "if a war starts, the only way we're gonna survive is if we find a good place to hide. Then, when things quiet down, we can do some scouting behind enemy lines."

My mind raced. In a way, Stanton made sense. But in another way, he made no sense at all. How could we just disappear into the woods? We had no food. No supplies. Nothing. And how could we leave our families? "What about our folks?"

"Our dads'll all be fighting," said Stanton. "And the

Russians probably won't hurt women and little kids. But—"

"But we aren't little kids," said Cannonball, interrupting.

"What d'ya say, O.B.?" asked Nick. "You with us?"

I took a deep breath. I didn't know what to say. I wanted to be in the club, but there was more I needed to know. "What about equipment?" I asked. "You're gonna need all kinds of stuff."

Stanton smiled and pulled a long strip of paper from his pocket. "We got plenty of equipment," he said, looking down at his list. "Four pup tents. Five canteens. Five knapsacks. Three penknives. Five flashlights. Rope. Matches. Compass. Six sleeping bags. Two waterproof slickers. Three boxes of K rations." He looked up. "We've been collecting supplies since things started getting bad in Berlin. Got enough stuff to camp out for a month."

"C'mon, O.B.," Nick urged.

Cannonball tapped my knee with his foot. "It's better than Siberia," he said gloomily.

I studied the faces around me. I didn't want to let the guys down. Not at a time like this. "Yeah," I said. "I'll join."

"All riiiight!" Cannonball shrieked. But this time Stanton did not scold him.

"Good," said Stanton. "Now we just gotta find the right place for a camp. We haven't found it yet."

"It's got to be close," said Nick. "And there has to be plenty of cover—and water."

"And it can't be near the restricted area," said Cannonball. "That place gives me the creeps."

I listened to my friends and I could see in my mind the place they were describing. A place where the thick green woods would provide shelter. A place where a shallow stream would bring clear, fresh water. A place far enough from the hill that it would be safe to walk. They had never been there, but I had. The pond. "I—I know a good spot," I said.

"Where?" Stanton demanded.

"Outside the village. Away from the hill."

"Is there water?" asked Nick.

"Plenty. A stream and a pond."

Cannonball beamed. "I told you guys he'd be a good soldier. I told you!"

Stanton leaned his back against the foundation wall and fixed his eyes on me. "How do you know 'bout this place?"

"I've been there."

"I mean, how'd you find it?"

I felt a lump form in my throat. How could I answer Stanton? How could I say anything about the pond without mentioning Claude? "Someone took me there," I said at last.

"Who?"

"Who?" I repeated dumbly.

"Yeah, who?" said Stanton.

I hesitated. I could lie. But what good would that do me? Everyone knew that only people from the village were familiar with the woods. And Stanton would surely know that there was only one person in the village who would have taken me. But if I told the truth—Claude was right. I had become so afraid of what others would think I had stopped thinking for myself. I had stopped *listening* to myself. "Claude took me," I said, shrugging.

Cannonball winced. "Jeez, O.B., I told you to stay away from him." He turned to the others. "I *told* him not to go near—"

"It's okay," said Stanton. "If he didn't go with Clod, we wouldn't even know about this place." Stanton's eyes found mine. "O.B., stay away from him, okay?"

I held Stanton's stare, but I didn't answer.

"Okay?"

"Yeah, he says okay," said Cannonball. "He says okay."

Stanton pushed himself off the ground and rubbed his hands against each other. "Where exactly is this place?" he asked, glancing down.

"There's a field on the other side of the village," I said. "It's got a broken tractor in front of it."

"I know where that is," said Nick.

"There's a path across the field that goes into the woods," I continued. "I'll show you from there."

Stanton nodded. "Good. I got to go somewhere this afternoon. So we'll meet here tomorrow at ten-thirty sharp. O.B.'ll be our scout. Okay with you, O.B.?"

"Sure," I said. "I'll be here."

26

It was the noisiest night I could remember. It was as if every car and Jeep on the base had taken to the roads. Horns blared. Brakes squealed. Trucks rumbled. And, in the distance, helicopter blades thwacked angrily at the humid air. They were all sounds I had heard before. But never so loudly. Never like this.

I climbed from my bed and pressed my cheek against the window frame. The base road had become two sluggish streams of headlights, each moving in a different direction. I followed with my eyes the strand of lights that traveled toward the village.

Since the meeting with the club that morning, I had tried mightily to push Claude from my thoughts. But no matter how hard I tried, something continued to gnaw at me, to tear at my insides. The pond. Claude's pond. The one place he felt at ease. The one place he loved above all others. The one place no other American knew about. Earlier, I had thought only of Berlin and finding a safe camp, but now . . . now I wondered. Was I about to give the club something that was not mine to give?

I turned from the window and wandered out of my bedroom. As I made my way down the hallway, I could see my mother in the living room, her legs curled beneath her on the couch, a thick book spread across her lap.

"Terry," she said, looking up, surprised. "I thought you were asleep."

"It's too noisy."

My mother nodded. "It sounds like those trucks are coming right through the house."

I crossed the room and slipped into my father's chair. "Dad coming home later?"

"I don't think so. The base is still on alert."

I ran my hand along the side of the chair until I felt the release for the leg rest. I pulled the wooden handle, and the leg rest sprang up. "I'm going to sit here for a while," I said, settling in.

My mother smiled, then returned to her book.

"Mom?" I asked after a minute.

"Hmmmm?"

"Can I ask you something?"

"Of course."

I stared straight up at the ceiling and tried to put my thoughts into words. "Have you ever given away a secret—or a secret place? Something like that?"

"Given away a secret?"

"Yeah."

"I suppose I have, at one time or another."

I glanced at my mother. "But what if you knew that it was going to make someone feel bad?"

My mother closed her book and placed it on the coffee table. "I think keeping a secret is part of being a good friend," she said. "It's an honor to know that someone trusts you enough to confide in you. To tell you something that they wouldn't share with anyone else in the world." My mother paused. "The only time I would not keep a secret is if it involved something that was wrong or dangerous. Does that answer your question?"

I nodded.

"Is everything all right, Terry?"

"Yeah," I said quickly.

I stayed in my father's chair and watched the shadows play across the ceiling. My thoughts pulled back and forth across my mind like a rope in a tug-of-war. On the one side, there was Berlin. And Stanton's plan. Four boys would hide in the woods and fight a guerrilla war. The more I thought about it, the sillier it seemed. We wouldn't last three days in the woods. Cannonball wouldn't last three minutes once the rations ran out. On the other side, there was Claude. It was just as my mother had said. He had honored me by confiding in me and sharing what was most important to him. The last thing he would have wanted was to have Stanton and Cannonball chase him from his pond.

But I had already made my promise to the club.

I turned the side handle on the chair, and the leg rest dropped with a jolt.

"Going back to bed?" my mother asked.

"Yes."

"Are you sure there isn't anything you want to talk about, Terry?"

"I'm sure." I knew my mother wanted to help. But the decision was mine now. I leaned forward and felt the soft cushions give way as I stood. I hesitated, then said, "G'night, Mom."

"Good night, Terry." My mother reached for her book. "Whatever it is, I know you'll work it out."

"I know."

I retreated to my room and sat on the side of my bed by the window. As I gazed out into the night, I felt a terrible feeling of sadness. I thought of Cannonball and the others sitting in the shadows of the pillbox. C'mon, O.B., they had urged. Join us! I thought of Claude, turning his back to me in his doorway. "I don't want to talk to you," he had said. "Not until you're ready to be my friend."

Friends. Who were my friends? My real friends? Who would stay with me if I never made a team or got a hit? Who would stand up for me? Who would never apologize for me? Who knew me better than anyone else?

I knew. There was only one answer. I would not—I could not—take the club to the pond. Claude's pond. I would not betray my friend again. If the guys wanted to learn the secrets of the woods, they would have to ask

Claude himself. And I would tell them that at the pillbox in the morning.

My eyes shifted to the base road. It was just as busy as before, but for some reason, the noise did not bother me anymore.

27

A quarter past ten. Only fifteen minutes till the meeting at the pillbox. I stepped back from my dresser to inspect myself in the oval mirror. My pale green shirt was the color of the summer leaves, my brown shorts the hue of a forest trail. Even the dark leather of my belt could pass as camouflage. I looked like the scout Stanton and the rest of the club wanted me to be. But I would not be their scout today.

My eyes lingered in the mirror, and I felt a cramp squeeze my stomach. I wished the meeting were over. That I had said what I had to say. And I wished I knew how the guys would respond. Would they speak to me again? Would they even look at me? I took a deep breath, pulled open my door, and followed the hallway to the living room. I could hear my mother moving about quietly in the kitchen, preparing for the new day. In the background, a deep voice droned on the radio. I could not make out the man's words, but I knew what he was talking about. Berlin. It was all anyone was talking about.

"Mom, I'm going out for a while," I said, poking my head into the kitchen.

"One minute," my mother said. She set a stack of dishes on the counter, then leaned toward the kitchen radio to absorb the last words of the news report. "The Russians haven't tried to block our access to West Berlin," she said when the announcer had finished speaking. "I guess that's a good sign."

"Yeah," I said.

"Now, where are you going, Terry?"

"To see the guys."

"Make sure you—"

The tinny buzz of the doorbell clipped my mother's words. "I'll get it," I said. "It's probably Cannonball."

I rushed to the front door and yanked it open. "Hey, Can—" I stepped back, almost jumping. A tall man, thin as a splinter, stood in front of me, his bony fingers clasping to his chest the wide brim of a felt hat. He was dressed all in black—shirt, pants, jacket, and shoes—and a stiff white collar circled his neck. "Father Quinn?" I asked.

"Morning," said the base chaplain, bowing his head.

"Morning," I replied. I did not know what else to say. I had talked to Father Quinn after mass, but I had never seen him away from the chapel before. He looked so different now, without his vestments—so out of place. I stood awkwardly at the door, not knowing what to do.

"Father Quinn!" my mother called from behind me.

"Come in!" She scanned the living room, making sure that everything was in its place. Then she hurried forward and took the priest's hat. "Please sit down," she said, motioning toward my father's chair.

"Can only stay a minute, Mrs. O'Brien," said Father Quinn as he settled in. "I'm stopping by some of the houses to say a quick prayer for the resolution of the problems in Berlin."

My mother nodded and grasped my arm. "Father, you remember my son, Terry?"

Father Quinn nodded. "Yes, of course. How are you, Terry?"

"Fine," I mumbled.

"Would you like some coffee, Father? Or tea?" my mother asked.

Father Quinn pretended to think it over. "Maybe a little tea, if it's not any trouble."

"No trouble at all," my mother said, turning back toward the kitchen. "I have the kettle on the stove."

I looked at my watch. Ten twenty-five. Only five minutes to the start of the meeting. I *had* to get going.

Father Quinn gestured toward the old rocking chair across from him. "Have a seat, Terry."

I lowered myself reluctantly onto the hard wood, sitting near the edge so I could spring forward and escape quickly.

"How long have you been here now?" Father Quinn asked.

"Two months," I said curtly. I didn't mean to be rude, but I did not want the conversation to go on.

Father Quinn pressed his lips together. "And you're going to be in the seventh grade?"

"Eighth," I said. I lifted a smoky gray ashtray from the high table near my chair. I turned the polished glass over in my hand and pretended to study the manufacturer's mark. I could feel the priest's eyes, watching me. I felt guilty about being so impolite. But there was no other way. Maybe another day I would talk more with him.

"Do you know a boy named Cannonball?" asked Father Quinn.

"Sure," I said, my eyes shooting up. "How do you know him?"

Father Quinn chuckled. "He used to be one of my altar boys. Until he grew out of the cassocks."

There was a rattling of fine china at the kitchen doorway. I looked over my shoulder, relieved. My mother was making her way into the room, balancing two cups and a plate piled high with sugar cookies on a fancy serving tray. She placed the tray on the coffee table and took a seat beside me.

I glanced again at my watch. Almost ten-thirty. Everyone had to be at the pillbox by now. I needed to see them—to tell them I would not be part of their plan. I drummed my fingers on my knee. I had to leave! Now! I pulled myself out of the rocker, stepped forward, and snatched a cookie from the tray. As I returned to the chair, I whispered in my mother's ear, "Can I go now?"

"After Father's prayer," my mother said in a voice meant for my ears alone.

I slumped back into the rocker. Father Quinn must have thought it was a cue to begin talking. He chatted on about the base, the school, the religion classes, and the parent volunteer program. And every time he seemed to stop, my mother would ask him another question. I watched glumly as the minutes ticked by. Ten thirty-five. Ten-forty. I could almost see the guys at the pillbox, peering over the crumbling walls, searching the recreation field. I could almost hear them, wondering aloud where I was on so important a day.

Finally Father Quinn put down his cup, stretched his legs, and pushed himself from the cushions. "Will you please join me?" he said.

I jumped to my feet. I folded my hands and lowered my eyes respectfully.

"Lord," Father Quinn began, "You who watch over us and protect us from all evil, You who control our destinies: we pray that You guide the hearts and minds of those in conflict over Berlin. We pray that this crisis will be resolved peacefully and that this family will remain safe and well." Father Quinn paused. Then he said, "Amen."

"Amen," I repeated. I did not wait for the priest to leave. I did not even look at my mother. I bolted from the room like a hound on a chase and flew through the back door. I ran as fast as my legs would carry me, and I did not stop until I reached the barbed wire fence by the base road.

I could see the pillbox now, clinging low to the earth, as if it were hiding from me, but there were no signs of life. No noise. No shadows. No movement. I squeezed under the bottom strand of wire, snagging my shirt on a rusty barb. I struggled to free myself, then sprinted the final yards to the tiny fort. The pillbox *was* empty. The club had gone. But where? I kicked angrily at the overgrown grass. As I turned away, my eyes were drawn to a patch of dirt near the entrance to the fortification. Two words had been scratched in the soil: GONE AHEAD.

28

The tractor sat old and broken, leaning heavily to one side as if sinking into the brittle grass. It seemed almost sad, resting there alone, its metal a dull brown and orange, its wheels twisted, never again to roll. I leaned my bike gently against the rusty hulk. Then I searched the narrow trail that snaked to the woods. There was no sign of the club, but the pond was still a distance away. If I could just find the guys before they reached the water, maybe I could turn them back or lead them to a different place. Maybe I could convince them that Americans were not allowed.

I brought my legs to a run. I *had* to find them. And fast!

As I sprinted down the trail, the woods grew larger, and the shapeless mass of the trees became a tapestry of dark trunks, bony boughs, and long sheaths of green. In the opening where the path met the forest, the gold light of the sun dissolved in a dusky dimness. I plunged ahead, out of the summer's heat and into the cool quiet of the woods. I ran as if on an obstacle course, dodging a rock here, hurdling a stump there. From time to time, a vine or branch would slap at my leg, warning me to slow down and marking my skin with angry red lines. But I ran on. On until my legs cramped and my chest ached. On until I reached the clear waters of the stream.

I hunched over, my hands on my knees, gasping for air. For a moment, I could not find the strength to move. I could do nothing but listen to the gentle murmur of the flowing water on the polished stones. Finally I dipped my fingers in the cool water and splashed my face and neck. It was time to move on.

My eyes fell again to the path. There! On the far side of the stream. Footprints! I leaped over the water and dropped to one knee. The prints were fresh and deep and were marked with wavy ripples. They told me everything. Boys wearing sneakers had come this way. And the only boys who wore sneakers lived on the base! I cupped my hands. "Stanton! Cannonball!" There was no reply, not a sound. It was as if the woods had swallowed my words.

I started off again. Past a tangle of slender saplings. Past the place where the trail split. I had to be close now. I had to— I stopped. Up ahead, where the trail turned toward the rise, my eyes caught a movement, a flicker of life somewhere between the trees. I held my breath and listened. There was a faint scuffling on the trail, not the random noise of an animal moving, but the regular, deliberate steps of a man.

I started to call but stopped. Something was not right.

If the guys were returning from the pond, I would hear their talk, their laughter. But there were no voices now. Only the sounds of a single person, walking. I stepped off the trail and slipped into the shadows of a towering oak. A stubby stick lay near my feet. It was not much of a weapon, but it was solid and its broken tip was sharp. I picked it up and held it closely to my leg, just in case. For the first time, I realized how alone I was.

The footfalls were growing louder, and closer. I peered around the tree's thick trunk, not too far, but far enough that I could see the trail. The seconds dragged painfully on. I could tell by the crunching of leaf beneath foot that whoever was coming was almost near enough to touch. I clenched my stick so tightly the rough bark burned my palm. I could see a foot, a leg, a— I blinked. It couldn't be. "Claude!" I said.

Claude locked in his step as if he had been sprayed with ice.

"Claude!" I said again.

Claude found my voice, and his head jerked in my direction.

I stepped out from the shadows and dropped my stick.

"O.B.!" Claude said. "What are you doing here?"

Claude's voice quavered, but it held no anger. Not at me. Not at anyone. It didn't make sense. If the guys had found Claude at the pond, they would have thrown him in the water for sure. He would have retreated, embarrassed and upset. But here he was, his towel draped around his neck, walking along the path, not mad at all. "I was just going up to the pond," I said.

"To see me?"

"Kind of," I lied. "Was anyone else up there?"

"Like who?"

I shrugged. "Like Stanton and the guys."

"Why would they be there?" Claude asked, puzzled. "They don't even know about it."

"Yeah," I said quietly. "They know." I looked down. There was so much I wanted to say—about Berlin, the club, the plan to build the camp in the woods. But I said nothing. Claude had not been a part of it. And he never would have understood.

"So that's why you're here? To meet them at the pond?"

I raised my eyes, and I could see the pain in Claude's gaunt face. "No," I said quickly. "I told them about the pond because of Berlin and everything. I was going to take them there, but I changed my mind. They came ahead to find it themselves. I just wanted to stop them."

Claude watched me through sad eyes. "Why did you change your mind?"

"Because . . ." I shrugged. "Because you're my friend."

Claude stared at me for what seemed the longest time, his head tilted slightly to one side. Finally he said, "They aren't up there, O.B."

"But I saw their footprints."

"Where?"

"By the stream."

Claude's face darkened. "You told them to stay away from the other trail, right?"

I swallowed hard. I hadn't given any directions to the club. I was the one who was to have led them. My eyes met Claude's, and he knew.

"O.B., they're walking straight for the hill."

My head began to spin. "We better go back and get help."

"There's not enough time," said Claude. "*We* have to stop them!"

29

"Stanton!" Claude listened to his voice fade into the vastness of the woods. "Stanton! Cannonball!" He shook his head grimly. "They're never going to hear us, O.B. The trees close in the sound."

I nodded. The woods by the trail to the hill were even more dense, more impenetrable, than by the trail to the pond. The trees were packed in tight knots, their trunks stiff and straight, their limbs reaching, stretching, as if to embrace one another. They formed living walls beside us and a dense canopy above, hemming us in and channeling us like mice in a maze. "How far to the restricted area?" I asked.

"Maybe two kilometers. I've never been that far."

"Is it marked?"

"Don't think so," said Claude. "Near the roads they put up signs that say *'Terrain Interdit.'* But not back here. 'Cept for the demolition men, no one goes up there."

Claude squinted down the path. "Come on. We'd better hurry."

We pushed ahead, side by side, runners in a dash toward an unseen finish line. And as we ran, I grew more angry and afraid. Why had the guys gone ahead without me? And why had they taken *this* trail? I had wanted to lead them away from the pond. But not in this direction. Couldn't they see that this trail was different? Couldn't they see the branches and wild grass fighting to reclaim it? Couldn't they feel the danger?

I glanced at Claude. His eyes were fixed on the ground, and his body jerked with each movement of his legs, like a new colt trying to run. He looked odd and awkward, but somehow he appeared at ease here, in the woods. More at ease than at the ball field. More at ease than in the village itself. Maybe this was the one place where he didn't have to be French or English or American.

The trees became a blur of brown and green as we rushed on, and though I could feel my body moving forward, there was a strange sameness to the woods. What lay ahead of us looked exactly the same as what lay behind us. It was as if we were running on a treadmill—moving, but not really moving at all. As we reached a soft bend in the trail, Claude slowed and shouted, "My *grand-père* came this way." He swallowed. "They used this path for reinforcements during the battle."

It was hard to imagine. Soldiers had come this way once, thousands and thousands of young men. *"Ils ne passeront pas!"* they had vowed. They would not let the

Germans pass. I could picture Monsieur LeClair as a young man, marching proudly in his blue uniform, his heavy rifle slung over his shoulder, his face shaded by the narrow brim of his crested helmet. What thoughts must he have had as he walked toward the hill, of family and friends, duty and honor? What fears must he have fought? Could he have guessed how few men would survive? Could he have known that this hill would become a grave?

The touch of Claude's hand on my arm pulled me from my thoughts. There, ahead of us, no more than twenty yards away, the trail split again. Two paths, choked with heavy scrub, threaded farther into the woods.

Claude came to a stop and sucked in a breath. "This is bad," he said.

"What do you mean?"

"These are feeder paths. My *grand-père* told me that when they brought up the reinforcements during the battle, they didn't want all the soldiers together in case there was an artillery barrage. So they broke them into groups and made them take different trails. That way at least some would live."

Claude did not need to say more. We were near the battlefield now, close to the forbidden area. That meant that Stanton, Nick, and Cannonball were, too. Only they didn't know it.

"We're going to have to split up, O.B."

I struggled to stay calm, to keep the beat of my heart from stampeding. I did not want to go on alone.

Claude pointed to the feeder trail to my right. "You want that one?"

"Guess so."

"Go down maybe a hundred meters," said Claude. "No more. If you can't find them, come back. I'll do the same on the other path. We'll meet here in a little while. Okay?"

"Okay."

Claude started off, this time at a hurried walk. He took several steps, then turned. "O.B.!"

"Yeah?"

"Be careful. Watch out for anything rusty. And don't ever leave the trail."

I nodded. "Claude, thanks for helping me."

Claude forced a smile. Then he vanished farther into the woods.

It was my turn now. I had to go on. I had to be as brave as the soldiers who had once fought here. I had to be as brave as Claude. I moved forward on the feeder trail, stooped like an old man, my eyes searching the ground for—for anything. It was hard even to walk. Brush clung to the trail in tangled mats, grabbing at my shoes. Branches, long fallen, formed bristly barricades that blocked my way. The woods seemed to be warning me, urging me not to go on. And for the first time, craters began to appear, gaping dents in the earth where shells had once landed. They told me that I was near the hill and that the ground was dangerous.

The sight of the craters pushed me to the center of the

trail. I walked as if on a tightrope, afraid to lean to the left or the right. My eyes began to play tricks on me. Was that a piece of bark on the trail? Or a patch of rust? Was that a stick? Or a rifle barrel?

I stopped in mid-step. How far had I gone? Fifty meters? A hundred? The woods seemed less dense here; I wondered if the shelling had thinned the trees. I peered down into a crater next to the path. It looked as if a giant had dug his fingers deep into the earth and scooped the soil. Tufts of wild grass struggled up from beneath layers of pointed needles and clawed at the sides of the hole. Near the center of the crater, moss stained a large rock exposed by the explosion. I turned back to the trail and peered ahead. I could not see where the trail ended, but I could almost feel the hill, looming ahead, watching me. I brought my hands to my mouth. "Stanton! Cannonball!" There was no response. Nothing but an angry robin, swooping low, chiding me for my rudeness.

Just a few more yards. That was as far as I would go. As I coaxed myself over a small bush, something hard met the sole of my sneaker. I froze. Was it a shell? A bomb? Slowly, carefully, I lifted my foot. As my sneaker left the ground, the mouthpiece of a rotting canteen emerged beneath it. I stepped back and felt another lump. This time, the tip of a rusty bullet protruded from a clump of wild grass. I fought to control the sick feeling that filled my stomach. The guys were not up ahead. They would have answered me. I had to go back!

30

I watched as the ant struggled beneath the heavy load it carried. It plodded across a clear patch on the trail, stopped, pulled to the right, then stopped again. It seemed not to know where it was going. I shook my head. Lost. It was not the only one. The ant probed ahead through the canyons and ridges that creased the dirt, until it found safety in the shade of a brittle brown leaf.

Over twenty minutes had passed since Claude and I had taken our separate paths. Over five minutes since I had returned to the meeting spot. Claude should have been back by now. Go only a hundred meters, he had said. But how far had he gone?

Horrible thoughts filled my mind. I tried to push them away, but I could not. I could see the hill swelling from the earth like a fresh grave, its slopes littered with the remnants of war. I could see Claude, lying hurt in a mossy crater, calling my name. I shook my head to chase the thoughts away; they remained, real and terrifying. No matter how much I wanted to, I could not stay here, waiting. Now there were four boys to be found.

I pushed myself off the ground and breathed deeply. Then I set off down the feeder trail that led to the left—Claude's trail. I walked cautiously. I knew all too well what lay ahead.

Claude's path was even narrower than the one I had taken, three feet at the widest point, no more. Otherwise it was much the same—the slithering roots, the clawing branches, the woven mats of twigs and grass. I pressed on, measuring each step, each movement, knowing that every yard I put behind me brought me one yard closer to the hill. And in the fierce silence of the woods, I began to wonder. Had I sent Claude on a wild-goose chase? What if the guys had not come this way at all? What if they had crossed the stream and doubled back? What if—

A noise! Not near me, but somewhere ahead on a part of the trail I could not see. I stopped and strained to listen, but all I could hear was the pounding of my own heart. Were my ears playing tricks now? No! There it was again! Closer this time—a muffled tramping, like soldiers on a march. It had to be! "Claude!" I screamed.

For a moment, the woods did not give up a sound. Then a high voice filtered through the trees. "Oh Beee!" came the reply.

I clenched my fists at my sides to keep them from shaking. My knees felt weak, almost ready to give way. It was as if I had lost all my strength, now that I didn't need it. I stepped to the side of the trail, and waited.

Claude came first, his face drawn. Cannonball lumbered behind him, his body filling the narrow path. Then came Nick, smiling weakly. Stanton straggled behind, his face hard and sour. For a moment, no one spoke. Finally I blurted, "What happened?"

Claude looked away.

"Got lost," Cannonball said, puffing. "We were just wanderin' around up there." He turned to Stanton. "I *told* you we should've taken that other trail."

"It was spooky," said Nick. "We saw bones."

"Could have been animal," Cannonball offered.

Nick shook his head. "I don't think so."

Cannonball slapped his hand hard against Claude's back. "If it wasn't for old Clod, here, we'd still be up there."

"We would have found our way out," Stanton snapped.

"Yeah," said Cannonball. "Maybe by Christmas."

Claude grinned but he seemed almost embarrassed. "I have to get home," he said quietly. "I have to practice."

We fell in line behind Claude, single file, like ducks trailing their mother. And when the path widened, I stepped up beside him. "Where'd you find them?" I whispered.

"Off the trail. Near the slope of the hill." Claude caught my eye. "It's good I found them when I did."

I wanted Claude to tell them. I wanted them to know how lucky they had been. And how the boy they called Claude the Clod had probably saved their lives. But I knew Claude would say nothing. Not a word.

After a time, the trail spilled out onto the worn path near the stream. Claude pointed the way to the pond, but we did not go there. For now, Berlin was all but forgotten. The dangers of the woods were far more real.

We walked on until we reached the field where the broken tractor lay. As I stepped from the woods, the bright sunlight forced my eyes closed. When I opened them, Claude had disappeared. He emerged a moment later from behind a thicket, straddling the seat of his battered bicycle. He squinted and looked at us, as if deciding what to say. Then he leaned forward against the handlebars. "There's only one rule at the pond," he said solemnly.

"What rule?" Stanton asked.

Claude looked at me, then back at Stanton. "You can only throw me in once," he said, his lips curling up.

Stanton tried to hide the grin that spread like cracking ice across his face, but it was far too wide for his hand to cover. "Okay," he agreed.

Claude's eyes met mine. He nodded. Then he pushed his bike into a roll and his feet found the pedals. "*A bientôt*, O.B.!" he called without turning.

I watched as my friend bounced down the path toward the road that would take him to the village. I watched as the sunlight played on his hair and splashed across his shoulders. I watched, and as he grew smaller in the distance, I shouted, "*A demain*, Claude! Till tomorrow!"

It was far too dark, too cold, for the last day of August. It was as if fall had tried to slip in before summer had had its turn. A thick blanket of clouds had rushed in during the night, sealing the base beneath a great gray dome. Rain had fallen for most of the morning, starting and stopping abruptly, like music in a game of musical chairs. We had decided early on that the club's weekly meeting could not be held at the pillbox. So we drew straws to see whose house we would gather at.

I leaned forward and rested my arms on the sill of Cannonball's bedroom window. I stared past the recreation field toward the village. It sat lonely and somber in the rain, its roofs cutting a long silhouette against the drab sky. For almost two and a half months the base had been my home, but now I felt just as close to that tiny village in the distance.

"You see 'im?" Stanton asked.

"Not yet," I said, glancing over my shoulder.

Stanton hesitated. "You want me to start the meeting without him?"

I looked at my watch. "I told him two o'clock. He'll be here. He made it last week—and the week before." That was all I said, but it was not all I thought. What I thought was how little there was for the club to talk about, now that Berlin was becoming a memory. It was not that the problems there were over; they were not. The East Germans had started to build a wall through the city to keep their people from escaping to the West. But it was clear that the world was not about to go to war over it. And without the threat of war, the club had lost much of its purpose. Now only my friend's presence at the meetings seemed to make them worthwhile.

"Yeah, let's wait a couple more minutes," said Cannonball.

Stanton shrugged. "Fine with me."

As Stanton, Cannonball, and Nick huddled together to talk of football tryouts, I closed my eyes and strained to listen to the sounds beyond the house. I was not disappointed. Before the grandfather clock in Cannonball's hall had chimed twice, I heard the clanging and clattering of the ancient bicycle. I did not need to open my eyes to know that the newest member of the club had arrived. "He's here," I said, smiling. "Claude's here."

Author's Note

When I was a boy, my father was in the army. That meant moving to a new military base every two or three years. Massachusetts, New Jersey, Utah, Ohio, Japan, and France were more than just names on a map. They were my homes.

The summer of 1961 found my family at an American military base outside a small village near the French city of Verdun. We arrived during the crisis in Berlin and were part of an international contingent stationed in Europe to help keep the peace. Verdun had been the site of one of the most terrible battles the world had ever seen. During the First World War, German and French soldiers fought savagely there, and between three quarters of a million and one million men were killed, wounded, or gassed. Forty-five years after the great battle, remnants of the fighting were still strewn in the fields and hills surrounding the city. To this day, French bomb-disposal experts, *les démineurs*, search the old battlegrounds for live shells.

Although my three-year stay in Verdun provided me with many ideas for this book, it is a work of fiction. The story, the characters, the base, the village itself are all products of my imagination.